If Georgie had been in any doubt about Abe's identity, then his voice killed all those doubts stone dead.

It was a voice that had haunted her dreams for so long. In her head, she had played and replayed so many scenarios where she would hear that voice, turn around and walk toward it as unerringly as she once had.

She would be in charge...calm...not struggling to get her thoughts in order.

"You!" She fought back the prickle of tears. "It can't be. What are *you* doing here?"

Everything was in free fall.

Time slowed. She couldn't tear her eyes away from his and in a sickening rush, she was not just seeing into a past that had come and gone years ago but into a future that was irrevocably breaking down in front of her.

A unit. *Her* unit. Tilly and her. A team of two because that was what happened when you had a child and the dad was nowhere to be found.

Except here he was.

Cathy Williams can remember reading Harlequin books as a teenager, and now that she is writing them, she remains an avid fan. For her, there is nothing like creating romantic stories and engaging plots, and each and every book is a new adventure. Cathy lives in London, and her three daughters—Charlotte, Olivia and Emma—have always been, and continue to be, the greatest inspirations in her life.

Books by Cathy Williams

Harlequin Presents

The Italian's Christmas Proposition
His Secretary's Nine-Month Notice
The Forbidden Cabrera Brother

Once Upon a Temptation

Expecting His Billion-Dollar Scandal

Secrets of the Stowe Family

Forbidden Hawaiian Nights
Promoted to the Italian's Fiancée
Claiming His Cinderella Secretary

Visit the Author Profile page
at Harlequin.com for more titles.

Cathy Williams

DESERT KING'S SURPRISE LOVE-CHILD

HARLEQUIN®
PRESENTS®

ISBN-13: 978-1-335-56820-5

Desert King's Surprise Love-Child

Copyright © 2021 by Cathy Williams

This edition published by arrangement with Harlequin Books S.A.

For questions and comments about the quality of this book,
please contact us at CustomerService@Harlequin.com.

Harlequin Enterprises ULC
22 Adelaide St. West, 40th Floor
Toronto, Ontario M5H 4E3, Canada
www.Harlequin.com

Printed in U.S.A.

DESERT KING'S SURPRISE LOVE-CHILD

CHAPTER ONE

CROWN PRINCE ABBAS HUSSEIN glanced cursorily at the pristine paperwork on the conference table in front of him and signed with a flourish.

There was no need to check anything. Due diligence had been done by his fleet of lawyers, several of whom were around the table, already packing away their computers, ready for the flight back to Qaram.

Behind him, flanking either side of the closed door, two bodyguards had been patiently waiting for the end of the proceedings. It was a little after seven in the evening, freezing cold outside and, like him, they were probably looking forward to a return to sunnier climes.

He straightened and absently glanced at his watch. At six feet four, he dominated everyone in the room and none more so than the CEO who could not have looked more joyful at having just sold his hotel. It had once been a firm fixture with minor celebrities but now, like an ageing has-been film star, it was in desperate need of a revamp and a new role.

It was a mutually beneficial sale for both parties

and added to Abe's choice portfolio of boutique hotels, a sideline to the serious business of running his country, a small but wealthy and powerful kingdom.

He had been here in London for three days of non-stop work. Frankly, he could think of nothing he wanted more than to return to the comforts of the five-star hotel where he had rented one entire floor to house his personal entourage, so when Duncan Squire suggested that he take a little time out to enjoy some of the savouries they had made especially for his benefit, he had to stifle a groan of pure frustration.

'My chef is excellent. She's spent some time creating delicacies for you and your staff.' Clearly in awe of the much younger man, Duncan half bowed and took a step back as he said this. He avoided bumping into the wall behind him by only inches.

'Of course.' The bath he had been envisioning would have to wait, as would the stack of emails that had piled up during his absence from Qaram. His father, after a health scare four years ago, had firmly retired from active duty, convinced that he needed to rest in defiance of everything both Abbas and a team of highly respected consultants had said.

He pottered now, enjoyed tending to his orchards and tracking down art to add to his already bulging private collection. It was a sedate pastime and, in truth, he seemed content enough to retreat from the world and its demands. Unfortunately, it meant that the weight of running the country now fell squarely on Abbas's shoulders so time out was not a luxury he could afford, not when there was work to be done.

He frowned, dragged his thoughts away from his father and the discomfiting notion that having lost him once, many years ago, to the isolation of grief after his wife had died, he was now losing him again, this time to the fear of his own mortality.

He would do as required, politely pick at what was on offer and make his getaway as quickly as he humanly could.

Surely they couldn't still be signing on dotted lines? She'd been buried down here in the bowels of the hotel kitchen for the past couple of days, sending up drinks and snacks, and Duncan had faithfully promised that this would be the last day of working overtime.

Georgie looked at the clock on the kitchen wall, registered that it was nearly seven-fifteen and gritted her teeth with frustration.

She cast a jaundiced eye at the staggering array of delicacies she had spent the entire day concocting. They ranged from several different types of hummus to mini sliders and smoked salmon rolls with caviar. No continent had been left untouched because, as Duncan had repeatedly told her from the very first moment royalty had decided to buy the hotel, she had to pull out all the stops—because the way to a prince's heart might very well be via his stomach.

Georgie was less concerned about the Prince's stomach than she was about the fact that she needed to get back to her apartment and was so tired of hanging around, sending stuff up and making sure everything was picture-perfect. She had yet to meet the Prince, but she was already sick to death of the man.

Now, as she picked up Duncan's urgent summons to the conference room with the last of the tasty morsels she had prepared, Georgie stifled a sigh and eyed the unwieldy trolley that she would have to shove into the elevator because there was simply no other way of delivering everything that had been prepared.

Ever since she had started working at the hotel, she had seen the upsides. For starters, Duncan had employed her at a time when she would have struggled to find work and he had bent over backwards to be accommodating. The members of staff had warmly welcomed her. It was a small hotel in a niche part of London and the people who worked there were all young and creative and lively and Georgie had built up a fantastic rapport with them all.

But, realistically, Bedford Woolf Hotel was on its last legs. Its quirky, theatrical flamboyance now felt dated, belonging to another, more innocent, era. It lacked the refined sophistication of its newer, brasher neighbours. There was also no air conditioning and the décor needed drastic surgery—some lightly applied make-up wasn't going to do—and there was a certain desperation to the old-world charm Duncan had spent the last couple of years trying to cultivate.

Everyone, herself included, was overjoyed that some rich prince, from a country she had never heard of, had paid handsomely for the place and the fact that he would be keeping every member of staff on was a massive bonus.

So who was she to moan about delivering a bit of food before heading home?

She glanced at herself in one of the ornate mirrors in the corridor on the way to the lift, saw her reflection staring back at her, serious, thinner than she used to be, her brown eyes enormous in her heart-shaped face and her cropped hair spiking up in all directions, always determined to do its own thing. She was twenty-six years old and sometimes she felt absolutely ancient. Right now just happened to be one of those times.

Usually, she wore jeans to work. Why not when she was usually wrapped up in an apron? But in keeping with Duncan's mantra to them all to be *neatly attired*, she had forfeited casual today in favour of a navy-blue skirt and a white blouse and a pair of flat black pumps, which made her feel a bit like a flight attendant who had somehow lost her way and ended up in a kitchen, in front of a stove, slightly dishevelled with a few suspicious smudges of grease in unexpected places.

She spun away from the mirror and briskly made her way to the lift.

It was a heavy-duty contraption that slammed shut on her and shuddered its way up two floors to where the conference facilities were located.

Head down, Georgie knocked on the door and pushed it open, her face flushed with embarrassment.

She wasn't accustomed to front-of-house duties. Those were usually the domain of Marsha, who was tall, beautiful and chatty.

Georgie, always quiet and contained, enjoyed the kitchen, where she could concoct dishes and play around with food, leaving the patter to those who were more adept at it.

Opening the door, she was immediately aware of *people* and a lot of them. Lawyers, accountants, two beefy guys on either side of the door and, of course, the Prince himself, who had his back to her and was staring through the window.

She barely saw him. She just wanted to ditch the trolley and head for the bus stop but then Duncan spoke. He asked her to explain what was on the heavy silver three-layered trolley.

Georgie drew breath, looked up and two things happened at once.

The man by the window slowly turned around and she, in turn, glanced in his direction, eyes drawn to him because he towered over everyone else in the room.

The Prince.

His bloodline was stamped in the regal arrogance of his bearing and the cool, controlled command in those deep, dark eyes.

He was so tall and so ridiculously striking—his face chiselled perfection and forbiddingly beautiful.

So sinfully good-looking and so terrifyingly *familiar*.

Georgie blinked and knew that while one part of her brain was telling her that he just couldn't be the guy she thought he was, there was another part of her brain pointing out that his was a face that, once seen, could never be forgotten. Yet how could this be the same man? How? *Buying* a hotel? Not *working* in one? *How?*

She knew that everyone had stopped talking and she could feel eyes boring into her. Duncan nervously said something but it was just white noise because the only thing she was aware of was that man by the window, staring at her in silence.

Disbelief, incredulity and shock roared through her with the force of a freight train and, like a computer suddenly overloading on too much information, her brain made up its mind to stop functioning altogether. Her breathing became shallow and panicked as she began to hyperventilate and, with a gasp, she felt herself doing something she had never done in her life before.

She fainted.

When Georgie came to, she was on a sofa and surfacing to consciousness like a patient emerging from a coma. Where was she? *What was going on?*

Her brain was foggy. It seemed, from what she could see through half-closed, still-dazed eyes, that she was in one of the hotel bedrooms with its familiar décor reminiscent of an old Penguin classic novel. Cream walls with burnt umber dado and picture rails displayed framed classics by Virginia Woolf. The sofa on which she now found herself was the same burnt umber as the woodwork.

She vaguely knew that, by registering what was

familiar, she was putting off acknowledging what made no sense.

'Here, drink this.'

If Georgie had been in any doubt about the identity of the guy who had caused her to black out, then his voice killed all those doubts stone dead. She would have recognised that distinctive drawl in the middle of a crowded bar. It was deep and dark, with just the merest hint of something smoky and exotic.

It was a voice that had haunted her dreams for so long. In her head, she had played and replayed so many scenarios where she would hear that voice, turn around and walk towards it as unerringly as she once had.

She would be in charge—calm—not lying on a sofa with her skirt hitched up one thigh and struggling to get her thoughts in order.

She wriggled into a semi-sitting position and breathed raggedly as her wide and still disbelieving eyes collided with his.

'You!' She fought back the prickle of tears. 'It can't be. What are *you* doing here?'

Everything was in freefall.

Time slowed. She couldn't tear her eyes away from his and, in a sickening rush, she was not just seeing into a past that had come and gone years ago but into a future that was irrevocably breaking down in front of her.

A unit. *Her* unit. Tilly and her. A team of two, because that was what happened when you had a child and the dad was nowhere to be found. When the dad had disappeared without leaving a trace of himself behind.

Except here he was. Tilly's dad. Gone from the scene for years. Back now...and *a prince*. She stifled her terrified whimper but there was a rushing in her head and in her veins and she felt dizzy and nauseous.

Memories broke their banks and came at her in a surging flood. And to her horror, not all those memories were toxic. Intermingled were other dangerously unsettling ones of languorous nights spent together, their naked bodies merging into one with a sense of belonging that had felt so very right at the time. But it *hadn't* been right. It had been *all wrong* and she had lived with the devastating consequences of misreading a situation, had dealt with them, made peace with them. And now...

Now everything was in freefall.

'You know what I'm doing here.' He sounded as shocked as she felt. 'I'm buying this hotel.'

'I can't believe this is happening.'

'Believe it or not, nor can I.'

Abe had regained his self-control at speed but for a few seconds, as he had turned round and seen her, the shock had surely equalled hers. Never had recall been so vivid. The breath had left his body and the walls of the room had closed in until there were just two of them in a confined space, the only other intruders his memories of a past now gone.

He had seen the horrified incredulity in her eyes and it had mirrored his, but he was a man for whom emotion was always rigidly disciplined. He had broken eye contact, begun moving smoothly towards her, powered by some sixth sense he never knew he possessed, somehow instinctively predicting that she would faint and already knowing that he would make sure the room was vacated so that there were no witnesses to the conversation that would take place when she awoke.

'Where is Duncan? Where's everyone gone? How did I get here?'

'You should drink that water, although I can always get you something stronger. You've had a shock.'

'You haven't answered my question! And I don't need water! I need… I need…'

I need to find out what is going on.

The guy who had vanished into thin air four years ago hadn't been a prince. He'd been an ordinary guy, a guy she'd fallen head over heels in love with, just *an ordinary guy.* Her mind grappled desperately to fit pieces together that just made no sense and underneath the chaos and confusion was the blistering realisation that life as she knew it was over. They shared a daughter. This wasn't a bad dream and nothing was going to be the same, if only he knew.

'How can you be *a prince*?' she whispered. 'It's not possible!'

'This is a long conversation to have here,' Abe said tautly. 'I never thought I'd see you again but now that our paths have once more crossed, I should tell you that I am not the person you probably thought I was.'

'Oh, you've got *that* right.' She swung her legs over the sofa and was assailed by a sudden attack of giddiness. Everything in Georgie raged against being here.

Hatred, bitterness and the sour taste of all of her shattered illusions ripped into her with such ferocity that the four years since they had last seen one another could have been four minutes.

He'd gone. Left her. Walked away without a backward glance and with no forwarding address. No telephone number. No point of contact. Just disappeared into thin air, leaving her to struggle with a love she hadn't asked for but one that had swept her away with the force of a tsunami. Leaving her pregnant and alone.

She'd been a notch on his bedpost.

Through her devastation, that simple truth had been unavoidable. He'd used her and then, when he'd grown tired of her, he'd walked away and he'd left no clues behind so that she could trace him—and, oh, how she'd tried.

'You haven't changed,' Abe said on a rough breath, only the slight deepening of his tone advertising the fact that he was as shaken as she was.

'I don't want to be here.'

'There are people waiting outside. I have given them orders not to enter but they will be wondering what's going on.'

'I have to go.' She pushed herself up and brushed aside his hand when he moved to help her to her feet.

More than that, she had to think.

'You can barely walk in a straight line.' He raked

his fingers through his hair and brought the laser intensity of his focus back to her ashen face. 'Where do you live? Allow me to get you back to your place.'

'No!'

Abe was startled by her vehemence but then how could she be anything *but* angry with him? Bitter?

Unwittingly, his dark eyes roved over her face. She really hadn't changed at all. She still had that *something* that had once fired him up against all odds and held him captive. She was so slight with a slender, boyish frame and short, dark hair that framed an intensely pretty, heart-shaped face. Her eyes were a curious shade of light brown with flecks of green and her lips were full, the perfect Cupid's bow.

Even with those huge, almond-shaped eyes pinned resentfully on him and her mouth downturned with simmering antagonism, Abe could still feel the unwelcome intrusion of a libido that had been all too dormant for way too long.

He gritted his teeth, vaulted upright and sauntered to the window, from which he stared down at wet, dark bustling pavements and street lamps fuzzy against the steady rainfall.

He was here on business.

He wasn't going to complicate anything by trying to recapture what was in the past. That door had been firmly shut and he wasn't going to reopen it. He couldn't.

Even though she was still the biggest test to his resistance that he had ever had. It wasn't just the way she looked, so different from the women he had always dated in the past. It was who she had been. Irreverent, outspoken in her own special, reserved way. Intelligent and challenging. Strangely shy and yet not afraid of holding her ground. So she hadn't known who he was back then, hadn't felt the need to be subservient, but even now she knew he sensed that in that respect she had changed very little.

She had burned a hole in his life. So different from any other woman…

They had shared a scorching affair and his last truly liberating one before his father had fallen ill and the course of his life had changed for ever.

'Wait here,' he said on impulse.

'Why?'

'We should talk.'

Georgie stared at him in mute, resentful silence but she stayed put even though every instinct in her was telling her to run away as fast as possible.

'I need to get back home.'

'Fifteen minutes is all I ask. I return to my country in two days' time, after I've sorted the last remaining legalities of the hotel purchase. The way we parted company last time… Let's at least clear some of the air before I head back to Qaram.'

Georgie wondered what he could possibly say to her that could clear the air. But of course, even now, things would seem straightforward to him. He didn't know of the beautiful life they had created between

them. He didn't realise that nothing was straightforward any more.

In the days and weeks and months after he'd left
Georgie had gradually come to accept that he just
hadn't felt the same way about her as she had felt
about him. He hadn't seen her as 'relationship material', for want of a better description.

As she had tackled huge changes to her life she
had never, ever foreseen, she'd looked back and as-
sessed what she'd missed at the time, in the heat of the
moment. They'd never discussed the details of their
lives, never shared their surnames. They'd adopted a
'live for the moment' philosophy that had suited her
at the time and would have worked if only she hadn't
ended up wanting so much more.

Now a few more things fell into sharp relief. The
way the one-bed flat that she'd been renting when
she'd first arrived in Ibiza had always been used as
their base. She'd had no idea where he'd lived and he'd
been adept at swerving around awkward questions.
She'd assumed that he worked at one of the many
hotels that lined the long strip of beach because he'd
never denied it. He'd had a cool air of self-assurance
that had made him seem so much more mature than
his peers, but she'd just put that down to the fact that
he was from another country and had been brought
up differently. Although, in retrospect, those were
details that had also been kept from her.

Now it made perfect sense, all those missing bits.
He was a prince and she was a pauper and she was
never going to be relationship material for him.

Was that what he was so keen to talk about? Did he want to justify his disappearance?

He reappeared in the middle of her agonised deliberations and she blinked. It was frustrating that she still couldn't seem to look at him without being intensely aware of his sexual pull even though she knew that it was that damned innate magnetism he possessed that had sucked her in in the first place.

He dragged a chair over to where she had sat once again on the sofa and leant forward, forearms loosely resting on his thighs.

'What did you tell them?' Georgie asked flatly. 'I don't want any gossip circulating about me. This is a small place. People talk.'

'I told them you were still a bit shaken, probably run off your feet preparing for this visit. I said that I blamed myself for the situation and, that being the case, I would take a corner seat and stay while you gathered yourself. Least I could do. The less fuss everyone makes, the better. I assured your boss that once you were less woozy, I would ensure that you were safely delivered back to where you live. I assure you that there will be no gossip.'

'You were always good with words.'

'I never lied to you.'

'No?'

'Perhaps I would have told you the truth, but the fact is that I never enjoyed the company of a woman the way I enjoyed yours and to have told you who I really was would have put an end to what we had. I was selfish and greedy and I wanted you for as long as possible.'

'And then you left and didn't spare a thought for me,' Georgie said bitterly. 'I suppose, given what I now know—that you're royalty—it wouldn't have occurred to you that I might have had feelings, that I might have been hurt at being used as a rich boy's plaything and then discarded without a second thought.'

Abe flushed. 'We had fun, that's all. There was always going to be an end to it and I thought you understood that.'

Tears stung the backs of Georgie's eyes because how differently had they viewed the situation. Had he used her? Not in his eyes, clearly, because they had just been having fun, two ships briefly crossing paths on separate journeys to other destinations.

In his case—to rule a country and run around buying hotels. In her case—to face a life that had been utterly derailed.

'The least you could have done would have been to tell me that you were going,' she said coldly. 'Did you think that if you'd done the decent thing and said goodbye that I might have become annoying and clingy?'

'I...had to leave suddenly.' He raked his fingers through his hair and sat back.

'How convenient. You could have texted me, but I guess that didn't occur to you either. Why should it? It seems that you are a man who can do as he likes with the click of a finger and that included walking off without a word. I looked for you, you know. I spent ages asking around and in the end I gave up.' She thought of Tilly, beautiful, innocent Tilly, the result of a relationship that never was.

'I was recalled to my country because my father had had a heart attack,' Abe said bluntly. 'It was sudden and there was no choice in the matter. Yes, I could have texted you but there seemed little point. I had to go and I felt it better to sever ties completely, without needless post-mortems. I knew you would move on.'

As he obviously had, Georgie thought with a mixture of sadness and animosity. People moved on after brief flings. It was always harder when the heart was involved though, as hers had been.

'Your father,' she said quietly. 'Did he recover?'

'In a manner of speaking. Tell me how it is that you've ended up here, working as a chef in a hotel in London, when you had plans to continue with your art, to freelance as an illustrator. I know you worked in the kitchen at that hotel in Ibiza…did you suddenly develop a craving to change career course?'

Georgie stilled as the present met the past. She glanced at the clock on the wall. Time was ticking by and she had to go. He needed to know about his daughter but…not right now. She just had to work things out in her head first, work past the pain of knowing that he had abandoned her without a backwards glance.

'Things didn't quite work out the way I'd planned. What do you mean when you say your father recovered "in a manner of speaking"?'

'He recovered but has not been himself since that episode.' Abe hesitated and Georgie knew that he was uncomfortable with sharing anything private about himself.

'If you feel embarrassed answering, then please don't bother.' Her head was beginning to throb and she rubbed her temples. 'I wouldn't want to put you on the spot by asking you for any personal information about yourself,' she said somewhat sarcastically.

'He has retreated from public service,' Abe said abruptly. 'Hence the urgency of my departure four years ago. I am his successor and it fell to me to take over the running of my country while he recovered. I had no idea that my role would become a permanent one, as it has. My father has decided, in defiance of everything the doctors have told him, that his life is effectively over. He has always been very energetic but he has lost his ebullience. He is no longer the man he used to be and that saddens me.' He shrugged awkwardly. 'That's of no account. It is what it is. My point is that I had to leave immediately and I knew things would have come to an end for us eventually anyway.'

'I have to go,' she muttered.

'This conversation needs some kind of conclusion. And you're working here…you still haven't told me what happened.'

She shrugged and averted her eyes. She wished she could close them and pretend that none of this was happening.

'This hotel? It's been failing for some time, am

I right? How is it…? Your plans… I don't quite understand.'

Georgie reddened because somehow that felt like a personal slight. She wanted to tell him that it wasn't her fault. She surreptitiously glanced at the faded elegance of the bedroom. Scratch beneath the surface and signs of dilapidation were all too visible, and she suspected Abe would have done a lot of scratching below the surface before he decided to sink money into the purchase.

'What were you doing in Ibiza in the first place?' she suddenly asked, and she noted the discomfort on his face as he lowered his eyes briefly, lush dark lashes concealing his expression.

'I was buying a hotel to add to my collection,' he admitted without bothering to dress it up. 'In fact, we met by chance and because of you I ended up staying three weeks longer than I had originally planned.'

'Should I take that as a compliment?' Georgie asked acidly, but even as the words left her mouth she knew that bitterness wasn't going to get her anywhere. 'Forget that. In answer to your question about the hotel: yes. Things have been rocky for over a year. Longer. It seems that no one is really interested in a hotel that's small and charming, not when they can go to somewhere bigger and better equipped, never mind the fact that this hotel was home to the Bloomsbury set years and years ago. You'll fix everything here and paint over the character that no one is interested in and you'll get bookings by the dozen, I'm sure.' Then she offered a stiff smile. 'I apologise. I suppose I shouldn't be saying stuff like that considering you're now my boss.'

Under any other circumstances, that very fact would have already kick-started thoughts about handing in her resignation, but she knew that once he left the country he would not return, whatever the circumstances. He had left once without a backward glance. He would leave again.

'You may not have realised this, but I have saved your boss the unappealing prospect of having to let staff go. I have looked at the accounts of this place in some depth.' He paused and looked at her steadily and Georgie could feel those dark eyes boring into the very core of her. She was desperate to tear her gaze away but she couldn't and she licked her lips as nervous tension built.

She hadn't realised that Duncan had been planning redundancies but, of course, what choice would he have had? The place had been running on less than half full practically since she had started working there.

'I know how much you are paid. G Curtis—Head Chef. Had I known your surname I might have twigged.'

'You know how much I earn? That…that's none of your business!'

'Of course it is. Everything about the finances of this hotel became my business the second I decided to throw money at it. I know how much you started on here, which was a deplorably small amount, and I know that since then you have had all of two pay rises as you worked your way up the culinary ladder. You had big dreams when I knew you, Georgie. How have you ended up working for pennies in a place like this? Yes, it's charming but, when it comes to career paths, surely you must have known for some time that you were facing a dead end?'

'I...' Her face was burning. She thought about those dreams he had mentioned, the career illustrating children's books she had hoped for... She'd always known it would be tough to start with, but she'd made some connections before...everything had happened. She'd known the road she had mapped out and the one she had ended up going down, working as a chef, had never been on the map.

She felt ashamed and then was angry for feeling ashamed because being a chef was very creative and fulfilling. As Plan Bs went, it could have been a lot worse. Her thoughts were settling into some kind of order now. Perhaps the intense shock had begun tapering off. Perhaps horror had been replaced with a sweeping sense of the inevitable or maybe, deep down, she had always known that sooner or later those conversations she had visited in her head would actually happen because the guy who had broken her heart and stolen her faith in love would return like a storm sweeping in from the sea—a tempest blowing away everything in its path.

She could see the guarded curiosity on his face and resented it. *It was okay for some...*

'No need to explain but...' he hesitated '... I would really like to find out about why you have ended up working here. No, more than that… I want to explain in greater depth, Georgie…why I left the way I did. We all are faced with choices. I would like to explain mine.'

'There's no need,' she muttered sullenly.

'Let me buy you dinner.' He smiled faintly. 'You're thinner than I remember. You look as though you need feeding up. Wasn't Italian your favourite choice of cuisine? Pasta carbonara, if I remember correctly. One last dinner, Georgie, before I go. Wherever you want to go, I will take you. I realise I do not *need* to explain myself, but I would really *like* to. Take this. My card.'

Georgie was busy staring at the embossed card he'd placed next to her. His name. His number. A royal crest. Gold on cream.

'I'll understand if you won't let me deliver you back to…wherever you live. I know that you may feel that my presence in your house is an intrusion when you are obviously still resentful about how things ended between us after all this time.'

'Can you really blame me?'

'There are always two sides to every story.'

'No, Abbas, sometimes there's just the one side.'

'Have dinner with me.'

'So that you can try and clear your conscience?'

'Perhaps I, also, have thought about the past and what we had…'

Her heart jerked, a weakness she knew had to take second place to the cold business that lay ahead of her. She loathed the pathetic, desperate voice inside her that ached for him to tell her just what those thoughts had been.

Had he missed her the way she'd missed him, even when she'd resigned herself to the superficial role she'd played in his life?

'Consider it, Georgie,' he urged softly, rising to his feet but continuing to watch her. 'This time, let us part ways in peace.'

She would have loved nothing more than to have ripped up that card in front of him. Peace? Over dinner? Two adults burying hatchets? Did he think that they would part company with a solid handshake, a *'You must drop by if you happen to be in the area'* and maybe a kiss on the cheek? Did he? How far from the truth that was. Time and events had put paid to any such thing.

She watched in silence as he waited, head tilted to one side, before turning on his heel to head for the door, and as he opened it she caught a glimpse of his bodyguards, waiting outside for him, stoic and incurious.

The door closed with a soft click and she reached for his card, shutting her eyes as her fingers curled around it.

CHAPTER TWO

TWENTY-FOUR HOURS LATER, practically to the minute, Georgie was standing in front of the impressive five-star hotel where the Prince was staying.

There had been no need for him to tell her the name of the hotel because she'd known even before he and his entourage had arrived in London to finalise the details of the sale of the hotel. She'd been told that the food would have to be superb and she had dutifully done her own due diligence and scoured the hotel's menu so she wouldn't replicate any of their dishes when preparing the delicacies for his visit.

Of course, she could simply have called the number on the card, that *very special* card with its *very special* hotline number to the big man himself, but she had rejected that idea because the mere thought of it had made her feel sick.

Such a card was the very thing she had craved four years ago. Now it felt like an insult, something that cheapened her, something dished out with the arrogant pity of a guy who hadn't thought twice about leaving her and now wanted to set the record straight with his conscience by letting her know why.

Poor Georgie, with all her dreams of making it big in the world of illustration and all her high hopes and hard-won contracts... Where had it all gone? Down the proverbial...

Anyway, the thought of hearing that dark, dangerous voice down the end of a phone line had given her too much pause for thought.

Best to take the bull by the horns and just show up at his hotel because her morals were far too deeply ingrained for her to turn her back on what had to be done, even though what had to be done filled her with simmering panic and fear.

She had dressed for the part. Not quite office ready, but certainly not casual. The flight attendant had been replaced, she now thought, heading towards the hotel, by mourner at the funeral of a distant relative. Just enough decorum to pay her respects but no wailing or howling because she hadn't known the relative very well. Black knee-length skirt, black rollneck jumper—and a black cardigan on top of that because it was freezing—and black tights. Underneath the puffer jacket, she felt she was sartorially equipped for what lay ahead.

It was going to be the most difficult conversation of her life, one she had anticipated having years ago but since then she had moved on with her life, and now she was scared stiff of the unknown because she had no idea where this conversation would take her. She just knew first-hand what loss felt like. She had lost both her parents, so there was no way she wanted Abbas to stroll into Tilly's life, upend it, and then casually walk away again. He'd done that with *her*, hadn't he? Telling him the truth was the decent thing to do, for her the *only* thing to do, but she would need to make it known to him that there would be no room in the equation for someone unreliable and a prince from a faraway country carried the definite whiff of unreliability.

The guy who'd walked away without a second thought would definitely not be the man who was suddenly overpowered with a sense of duty to a child he hadn't asked for.

She would do what she had come to do and her conscience would be clear. He didn't have the monopoly on wanting a clean slate. But when she tried to imagine what she was going to say and how he might react, she felt the sickening twist of dread deep inside her and she had to remind herself that this was about Tilly; this was about their child and his right to know of her existence.

Head down, looking neither left nor right and definitely not behind to the entrance to the Tube and the temptation of flight, Georgie made her way into the hotel.

The call from reception came through just as Abe was about to phone his father.

Georgie. In the foyer of the hotel.

He tossed his cell phone on the leather sofa where he'd been sitting and strolled towards the bank of windows in his suite that offered extensive views of the City of London.

At a little after seven in the evening, it was dark and the city was like a blurry impressionistic artwork, washed out by the steady torrent of rain that had been falling since mid-afternoon.

She'd come. He hadn't realised how wired he'd been since he'd left her at the hotel with his card. Of course, there was no way he could have chased her if she'd decided not to take him up on his offer, but it would have left a sour taste in his mouth.

Seeing her again… Yes, he could understand her antipathy towards him. He'd left. No tearful good-byes or weeping and wailing. He'd done as he'd seen fit at the time because there had been no way the future he'd instinctively known she wanted would have been compatible with what Fate had chosen for him.

Everything in life came with its own limita-tions and subclauses and caveats—and his life came with more than the usual amount. Nothing was ever straightforward for him.

When he thought about that snatched moment in time in Ibiza, when there had only been the sea and the sun and Georgie and so much lust there were times he felt he might combust from it, it was like a glimpse of what normal life might look like. Nat-urally, he had not yearned for what lay outside his reach, but it had been…liberating and he had enjoyed every second of it and seeing her again now brought all those memories flooding back.

He remembered her youthful plans and felt intensely sad that those plans had come to nothing.

Why?

He realised she hadn't gone into any detail but that, in itself, told a story. Whatever had happened, she had clearly been too ashamed to tell him when he'd asked the day before.

He hoped she would confide in him now, perhaps over the dinner he had offered.

Abbas was surprised at how strong the urge was to talk to her, to try and be open with her about why he'd left the way he had, so that she would understand and forgive.

He could only think that some undercurrent of, yes, guilt must have stayed with him all these years and had been resurrected by her sudden reappearance in his life.

But where she had ended up...

He wanted to find out more.

He knew she likely struggled to make ends meet on her salary, her pay enough to keep body and soul together but without any frills. Cheap plonk but never champagne. He'd revisited the hotel's books since seeing her yesterday to remind himself of what she earned. She'd started out waitressing but her talent at cooking had soon been spotted, judging from that first pay increase a mere month after she'd joined, but even in the role of chef she still wasn't making a huge deal of money. The hotel was on its last legs— no one there earned that much because there wasn't enough to do the rounds.

CATHY WILLIAMS   35

How? How on earth had her dreams crashed and burned so spectacularly? The question kept coming back to him because it made no sense.

If she'd come here because in the cool light of day she really did want to hear his side of the story, then she would know that he wanted to hear hers.

He half closed his eyes and the image of her leapt into his head with graphic clarity.

So damned pretty...so sweetly tempting without ever realising it...

She'd come to talk and talk they would, but what if talking was not her only reason for being here?

He allowed his mind to drift, went back in time and enjoyed the memory of her, her slight body under his, so supple, so elegant and as graceful as a ballet dancer. There was nothing obvious about her and that subtlety had been an addiction. He had been mystified how someone could be so soft yet have such a fierce core, so shy yet sizzle with such allure...

What if she's come for more than just a meal and a heart-to-heart? a little voice insisted on whispering in his head and Abe very firmly closed the door on that notion. He hoped she hadn't because he didn't relish the prospect of gently showing her the door. Because whether he still found her attractive or not, he was not in the market for any kind of involvement, least of all with an old flame.

Abbas was well aware of what he brought to the table. He also knew what he didn't bring, and that was emotional involvement.

He couldn't. Experience had taught him that the

whims of emotion would never serve a crown prince. Only a cool head could do that.

But that aside, he'd seen how love could cause as much pain as it could create joy. He'd keenly felt the pain of losing his mother and lived through the horror of his father's anguish when he'd lost his wife. Abbas wasn't really sure whether his father had ever got over the loss of the woman he'd loved so much. He just knew that from every angle, it didn't work letting your heart take over the reins. He'd done Georgie a favour by walking away, he told himself. He'd spared her the pain of realising that he couldn't allow himself to offer her the sort of emotional connection she would have been looking for.

He stiffened at the rap on the door, moving to open it himself before one of the two bodyguards stationed outside could buzz to let him know of his visitor's arrival.

Outside Abbas's hotel-room door, Georgie was trying hard not to feel cowed by the presence of the same beefy bodyguards she had glimpsed yesterday. She was staring straight ahead at the closed door and doing her best to ignore the men on either side of her. In her mind's eye, she pictured Abbas and was dealing just fine with the obedient, cardboard-cut-out image in her head, but when he softly pulled open the door, she felt the breath leave her body in a whoosh.

He was in a pair of jeans and a dark, fitted long-sleeved tee shirt. Gone was the immaculate, hand-tailored suit of the day before. This was more the guy she remembered and yet, in a thousand crucial ways, nothing at all like him.

Her mouth went dry and for a few seconds, she couldn't think straight. In fact, she couldn't think *at all*. How could he still exert such a pull on her senses? When she knew him for what he was? A creep who had used her. He might have been summoned back to his country because of an emergency but, face it, he hadn't seen any reason to tell her as much because she'd simply been disposable. She'd reached her sell-by date and he hadn't thought twice about walking away.

So why the hell was she finding it so hard to tear her eyes away when her head knew how the land lay?

'You don't look surprised to see me,' she told him, chin up.

His eyebrows shot up. 'Would you like to come in before we begin this conversation?'

He stood back and Georgie swept past him, breathing in his scent.

'Drink?' He padded barefoot through to a living area that was bigger than her entire flat.

'Are you?'

'Am I what?'

'Surprised that I'm here.'

He paused and considered her with his head tilted to one side. 'Not entirely,' he admitted. 'You can take the jacket off, Georgie. I am no fan of the cold. The heating is on in here.'

He was still so beautiful, she thought resentfully. So tall, with tigerish gold-flecked eyes and perfectly chiselled features, stamped with the cool, superior confidence conferred upon him from his noble lineage.

She removed the puffer jacket and hesitated before taking the glass of wine he was holding out to her.

'That said,' he murmured, 'I anticipated some advance warning… A chance to book a table at a restaurant…'

'Dinner…' she said vaguely.

'Is that why you're here?' He shrugged but his dark eyes were intent under lush lashes. 'No matter. The room service is excellent. Will you leave it to me to order? And relax, Georgie.' He paused. 'We're just going to talk. You don't have to worry that there might be anything else behind my suggestion that you join me for dinner.'

'I'm not,' Georgie said sharply.

'Good.' He smiled. 'Tell me what you'd like to eat. No need for any menu. Whatever you want, they will oblige.'

'The advantages of being a prince,' Georgie muttered, feeling herself flush. 'I don't care. Anything.'

'Okay.' But his voice was cooler now, more speculative. He sauntered over to his phone, dialled what she expected was room service and ordered who knew what. She didn't listen and instead busied herself looking around the sort of expansive, luxurious space that only the ridiculously wealthy could ever hope to afford. Huge, ultra-modern kitchen, huge ultra-modern sunken sitting area with leather furniture, several doors ajar, probably leading to huge ultra-modern bedrooms and bathrooms. Everything, from walls to blinds to curtains, was in varying shades of off-white. It was clearly the biggest and the best the hotel had on offer.

'So…' he drawled, moving to sit on one of the leather sofas and looking at her over the rim of his glass. 'You're here and I am glad you decided to come, Georgie. I need not tell you that I've been curious as to what's happened with you since we last saw one another… Tell me what you've been doing…'

'You know what I've been doing,' she said tersely, edging her way towards one of the pristine white chairs and perching awkwardly on it. Surrounded by this lavish display of luxury, she was acutely aware of the gaping chasm between them. Sprawled on the sofa facing her, he was the epitome of sophistication. He *belonged* against this sort of backdrop, casually elegant and at ease in his surroundings.

She, on the other hand, looked as she felt—out of place and ill at ease.

'Tell me why you ended up where you did. What happened? When I knew you, you were so enthusiastic about illustrating. You were also good at it. I remember the sketches you constantly used to do.'

'Life happened,' Georgie said curtly, heart speeding up and nervous perspiration dampening her upper lip.

Abe nodded sympathetically and she gritted her teeth, willing to bide her time for the moment.

'It has a way of doing that,' he agreed. 'I never expected my father to fall suddenly ill the way he did—

the best-laid plans and all that… I also never saw myself taking over as ruler of my country at such a young age but, as you say, life happens and we simply have to adjust and go along for the ride.' He paused, frowned. 'There's no need to look so nervous, Georgie. No one's forced you to come here so I don't understand why you're so tense. Art and catering are worlds apart. Did working at that restaurant in Ibiza kill off your original plans?'

'I couldn't afford to invest in the time I would have needed to get contracts,' she told him jerkily. 'Yes, I had some connections but even with those… I would have needed to be able to financially support myself for a while in order to successfully build my business.'

'Quite,' Abe murmured with an understanding smile.

'I never told you,' she said quietly, 'but I went to Ibiza in the first place to recover from my father's death.' She watched as he registered surprise and she knew why because when they'd been an item, she had been the one doing all the confiding, but she had still been too raw then to tell him about her father's brief illness and sudden death.

Her mother had died when she'd been young, too young for Georgie to really remember much about her. Her father, the local vicar, had been the rock in her life. He had never remarried and so there had been no competition for his attention—it was always just the two of them. He had been a gentle man with a very firm moral compass and Georgie had spent her life striving to please him, to do well at school, then at art college, aware of but not unhappy with the expectations he'd placed on her.

She wondered what he would make of her situation now. Frankly, she worried he might be turning in his grave.

'I had to get away for a while, wanted to throw myself into a lifestyle that could…make me forget.' She waited for him to interject but he remained silent, looking at her with his head tilted to one side. He'd always been a good listener. That was something she remembered. He looked like a playboy, with those swarthy, impossibly sexy good looks, but he knew how to listen. It had been seductive, especially at a time when she had been hurting and vulnerable. He had shown her how to trust again, how to laugh again, how to see that there were always rainbows even if the skies looked stormy. She'd been ready to reveal that final snippet about herself to him, knowing that he would understand, would be there for her, would know just how to wrap her in the safety of his embrace…but then he'd vanished.

'I'm sorry,' Abe said quietly.

'Why?'

'I wish you'd told me.'

'Really?' Past hurt suddenly swamped her and she clenched her fists. 'Because you would have sympathised for five minutes before disappearing into thin air, without bothering to tell me?' She waved her hand and looked away. 'Doesn't matter. I was there… to recover. I needed to get away from everyone and everything. I grew up in a small village where everyone knew everyone else's business. It was stifling after my father died. The kindness, the sympathy... the pity, sometimes. I appreciated that people cared but I needed to escape.'

She shook her head, determined not to let emotion get the better of her. 'Anyway, why should you be interested in hearing all this now? The fact was that I ran away, used some of the money Dad left me to travel. That was how I was able to afford to rent that flat in Ibiza. When I returned, there was just about enough left to buy somewhere small...but there was no way I could contemplate months of living off my savings while hoping to make it big. Illustrating is a competitive business and... No, I couldn't take the chance of striking the jackpot, even though my list of contacts might have been enough to see me through. There was just too much uncertainty in going down that road. It would have meant sacrificing the chance to buy a place of my own and there was no way I could do that.'

She breathed in deeply and gazed down at the black void of a precipice. She had come here for a reason yet she was cravenly relieved when he picked up the conversation.

'Your father's death was unexpected enough to make your world unravel,' Abbas said with pinpoint accuracy, 'as my father's sudden heart attack caused my life to deviate from the direction in which it had been going. Similar situations, in some ways, would you not agree?'

* * *

Sitting here, Abe remembered with a pang how easy their relationship had been. He was surprised to learn about her father, but he could empathise because there were always some things a person found difficult to share. When he thought back to the girl she had been then, it made a curious kind of sense because he'd never thought she had the personality of someone who enjoyed the brash party life of that particular strip of beach where she'd worked. He'd first met her when she had blushed her way through an explanation of the paella she had cooked. He had insisted on the head waiter fetching her from the kitchen because the food had been so good and had been amused and tickled pink at her embarrassment.

It didn't sit well with him knowing that he had hurt her, even though, at the time, he had seen leaving as the most efficient way of ending something that had only ever been an exceptionally enjoyable fling. Whenever he'd thought of elevating it beyond that, he'd mentally put the brakes on, preferring to stick to what he knew, to adhere to his usual limitations. He'd known that going off-piste on that front could never be an option for him.

'I never expected my own father to have a heart attack,' Abe confessed. 'He had always been a strong man. The only time I remember him laid low was when my mother died. At any rate, it was a shock to be recalled to the palace out of the blue.' He hesitated. 'I did what I thought was best, Georgie.'

'Best for you, you mean,' she shot back.

'Best for the both of us. I never meant to hurt you. I never made you any promises, Georgie.'

'I'm not saying you did,' she said stiffly.

'My life has always been prescribed,' Abe said flatly. 'As an only child, I was relentlessly groomed to be ready to take over the duties of my father at any point.' He hesitated. 'My father had a very successful arranged marriage. He learnt vital lessons from his own father who had cast his net wide, had mistresses and eventually married two of them. My grandfather had no control over his behaviour and the country suffered as a result. Vital investments in infrastructure were sidelined, business of any sort was put on hold, money was squandered and we lost standing in the international community. It took a long time for things to be steadied and was in no small part due to the efforts of my father, who had the sense to rein in his private life. He married for convenience to a woman who knew the role she would have to play. Love may have come later for them, but suitability was the key factor to his choice of wife and there was never any question that I would have to follow in his footsteps. If I led you to believe that things were more serious between us than they were, then I sincerely apologise to you now.'

'You didn't lead me to believe anything,' Georgie denied. 'I over-invested.'

'You're a romantic. That is a road I have never travelled down and never will.'

'So you've said.'

'Which doesn't mean that I'm lacking in emotion...'

* * *

Georgie didn't know what was worse, the message or the messenger. In a minute, he would be reaching for a handkerchief so that she could dab her tear-filled eyes while laying it on thick with the sympathy.

'Like I said, I enjoyed what we had and after what you've told me… I understand it would have been a tough call choosing between a house and a career.'

'I'm not asking for your pity, Abe,' she said tightly.

'That's not what I am giving you,' he said, slowly rising to his feet before heading towards the well-appointed kitchen and returning with the bottle of wine. 'Pity and sympathy are two different creatures and they stem from two different standpoints.' He sat back. 'Perhaps this is the conversation we should have had four years ago,' he mused. 'Do you think the parting of ways would have been made easier? If you had told me about your father? If I had explained to you who I really was? That there could be no future between us? I am not a believer in retrospective wisdom, so it is good that the air has finally been cleared.' He reached across to top up her glass.

Georgie remained silent. 'No more wine, thank you.' He had ordered food and she'd completely forgotten about it until there was a knock on the door and a trolley was wheeled in and silver cloches whipped up by a fully uniformed waiter. A Chinese feast. Her mouth watered but she reminded herself that this wasn't a social visit. She would eat but she wasn't going to consider it sharing a meal with him.

She helped herself to the food and didn't look at

him as she ate. Despite the delicious smells it was emitting, it tasted like cardboard. How could she enjoy any of it when her stomach was churning and her mind was spinning cartwheels?

'The truth is always better than lies and subterfuge.' Georgie knew this to be a fact, but if she had known his true identity she would have run a mile. She might have been innocent, but she wasn't completely lacking in grey matter.

Yet, when she thought about *never* having had him in her life, her mind drew a blank.

Without this stranger sitting opposite her, there would have been no Tilly and Tilly was her unexpected heavenly gift that gave her life meaning.

Was it possible to sift through the strands of your past and pick out the bits you didn't like, or did cause and effect make that impossible?

'You never expected to ever run into me again, but you did, Abe. Maybe you feel guilty at the way things ended. Do you? Is that why you asked me out for dinner before you disappear to the other side of the world?'

Again.

Georgie knew that that was something she should not forget. He had disappeared with no warning. That was the kind of man he was. Programmed to end up with a certain type of woman and she was not that type of woman and never would be.

'Why should I feel guilty? Haven't I explained?'

'It doesn't matter.' She waved one hand impatiently. 'You're right, we can continue going round and round in circles but we won't get anywhere, because there's a reason I'm here and it's not because I feel any need for you to apologise. I don't. What happened, happened.'

Despite the disinterest she was displaying, Georgie had never hated anyone the way she hated him now. For disappearing, for stealing her heart, for showing up and glibly writing off what they had shared as nothing important, for asking her out for a stupid expensive dinner because he wanted to *salve his conscience*. She hated him for knowing what she had failed to see at the time: that he was completely out of her league. She hadn't been playing with a full deck of cards because she hadn't known who he was, how rich and important he was. She felt foolish now for not instinctively clocking what should have been obvious to anyone with half a brain. Even masquerading as Mr Ordinary, he'd still been so sophisticated, so self-assured, so good-looking. There, in Ibiza, she'd actually believed that she was a different person and not the girl next door she'd always been, but if she'd taken a few seconds to stand back, she would have known that there was no way he was going to hang around for ever.

Mostly, though, she hated him for showing her what she wanted to forget, for showing her that he still got to her, that her body could still react to him. She hated him for the dreams he had put in her head that would never have materialised.

'You asked me how it was that I ended up where I did, working at the hotel.'

'Your father died. If I had known that then, perhaps I would have told you who I was, would have—'

'Would have what? That's raking over old coals, Abbas. The past is best left alone. Let me fully explain why I ended up where I did. I could have worked something out with the illustrations if I'd really wanted, used up savings and maybe worked evenings so that there was some money coming in until I made a name for myself. I could have figured something out, but in the end there was no choice for me. Life had other plans in store. You see, I found out that I was pregnant.'

'Pregnant?'

He couldn't have sounded more shocked and his eyes lowered with laser-like intensity to her stomach.

'Pregnant,' he repeated, laughing shakily. 'Yes, I can see how that might have interfered with the future you had planned. And…the baby?' he asked after a brief hesitation.

'A daughter. I called her Matilda.'

'Nice name. And the father?'

His dark eyes remained pinned to her face but he felt a sudden surge of emotion at the thought of another man with her. *Touching her…inside her…fathering a child.*

He shifted because such raw emotion, springing from out of the blue, was not welcome. What they had enjoyed was in the past and, as she'd said, the past was best left alone. There was certainly no room there to harbour feelings of jealousy because she had moved on with another man. Any lingering sexual attraction he might still feel for her didn't make sense. In his well-planned and well-ordered life, he couldn't afford the chaos of emotion even though, and he was loath to admit it, seeing her again had fired up all sorts of memories and wayward thoughts that made him wonder whether he had actually put her behind him as successfully as he'd assumed.

Georgie didn't answer. Her hand was shaking as she reached for the bag she had brought, fishing out her wallet, from which she carefully extracted a photo to extend to him.

'Tilly is a little over three years old. That's her.'

'Attractive child.' He set the photo on the table next to him and looked across at her quizzically, wondering what it was about her that wouldn't let him shut the door completely on their past. 'But I admit I'm confused. Where is this going?'

Abe genuinely didn't know. For once his sharp brain had hit a roadblock and, search as he might, there were no clues on her face to offer any signposts as to what his next move should be. Why was she here? She'd picked at the food and been uninterested in any kind of catch-up conversation. This had not been the evening he had envisaged but in truth he wasn't entirely sure what he *had* envisaged.

Did she think that there were still the embers of a fire between them that could be stoked back to life? He'd tiptoed around that possibility, then closed the door by telling her that his offer of dinner had contained no hidden agenda, but had he not been clear enough?

Surely she couldn't be playing some sort of long game—it didn't tally with the girl he remembered, who had been so open, so honest and so lacking in guile, but then people changed and especially so when bitterness took the starring role. Had she sensed his weakness? Had she gauged, despite his best efforts, his infuriating temptation to touch what he used to be able to freely touch? He would have to disabuse her of any notion that they could pick up where they had left off, that playing hard to get wasn't going to stir his interest, but, for a fleeting moment, he felt the pull of something so powerful that he breathed in sharply and lowered his eyes, shielding his expression.

'I don't see a wedding ring on your finger,' he said abruptly. Perhaps the father had done a runner.

Had she come here to ask for money? he wondered. But he dismissed that thought as fast as it surfaced. Every instinct told him that this was not a woman with a begging bowl behind her back and every intimate memory reminded him that she had never been the sort to ask for anything.

'For a very good reason,' Georgie said in a low voice. 'Because I'm not married.' She shook her head impatiently. 'You really don't get it, do you?'

'Get what?'

'You probably don't remember but I got a stomach bug when we were…going out. Something I ate.'

'Sardines.' Abe frowned and then smiled and relaxed at the innocuous change of subject. 'I warned you not to have them. You can never trust the quality of the fish cooked in a pop-up restaurant on a beach. You were out of it for nearly two days.'

'I'm surprised you remember.'

'I remember everything about our time together,' he returned, shocked to find it was the truth.

Searching her face, Abe noted the flushed softening of her features and the flare of her nostrils and her sudden intake of breath and felt the atmosphere between them change, and this time the charge was sexual, firing him up and killing all of his good intentions to ignore the chemistry that was still lingering somewhere inside him. He shifted, gritted his teeth against the heaviness of a sudden erection that threatened to be all too visible unless he could manage some of the prized self-control he was so proud of.

Without either of them noticing, the distance between them decreased as she leant into him and he, in turn, edged towards her.

'Georgie…'

'Don't.'

'Don't what?'

'Don't look at me.'

Their eyes tangled and just like that every thought flew out of her head and Georgie was back to the past, back to the way she had felt when he had first touched her, as though she'd spent her whole life in deep freeze, waiting for him to come along and wake her up, like Sleeping Beauty and that kiss, minus the happy-ever-after ending. She'd run away to Ibiza to recover and she had found love, or maybe love had found *her* because she certainly hadn't been looking for it.

She would have turned away, but she could barely move. Recall of all the pleasure she had had at his touch slammed into her with shocking clarity and she felt the tightening of her nipples in hot response. Her tongue darted out and her lips remained parted as her eyes dropped to the wide, sensuous curve of his mouth, a mouth that had once devastated her body and set her aflame with desires she'd never suspected she was capable of feeling. He had shown her how to feel alive again. She had always marvelled that he had been attracted to her in the first place, when she'd known that he could have had any woman at the snap of a finger, but there had been no room for doubts or insecurities in her headlong, burning need for him.

Shaken, Abe dropped his eyes, unnerved by his visceral response to her.

'Why have you come here, Georgie?' he asked softly. 'I realise now that I inadvertently hurt you when I left Ibiza without discussing it with you; in hindsight, I probably should have told you I was leaving. But you do understand that, ultimately, I would still have had to go. Is it that you think we may be able to reignite what we once had? I cannot change the past or the present...or indeed the future, as it is not mine to command. I have a country to lead and you have a child to care for now, do you not?'

He clenched his fists, suddenly frustrated beyond

all bearing because, despite every word leaving his mouth, he *still* wanted her. She was already beginning to make him long for things that were completely impossible and she'd only been back in his life for an hour!

'Are you mad? You think I don't know that if you couldn't contemplate a relationship with me when I was young, free and single, you certainly would never contemplate one with me now that I have a child?'

Of course he couldn't, but he genuinely didn't understand what was going on and so was clutching at anything that might make a bit of sense. Naturally, in his hunt to find answers, he was looking in all the wrong places.

'I've already told you, I looked for you, you know. Everywhere. After you'd gone. That's when I worked out just how much I'd invested in you emotionally, and just how little you'd invested back. You'd never had the slightest interest in us having any sort of relationship...'

'We *had* a relationship!'

'No, we had sex, Abe, great sex, and lots of it. Ask most women, and they wouldn't call that a relationship. And then you left and made sure I had no way of contacting you.'

'For reasons I thought were sensible,' Abe reiterated, spreading his hands.

'I get it. We came from different worlds. You, a prince...' She laughed shortly. 'It must have been a novel experience slumming it with me.'

'I don't like to hear you putting yourself down,'

he said sharply. 'Nor do I enjoy the implication that that's the sort of man I am.'

'But it *is* the sort of man you are!' Georgie cried helplessly. 'That's *exactly* what you did! You would *never* have considered anything serious with me because my background wasn't elevated enough. That's why walking away without bothering to tell me you were going was okay with you.' She sighed with angry impatience. 'It doesn't matter. I wanted to tell you and I couldn't find you *anywhere*. Heaven only knows why I'm here at all, but I suppose I still feel the same way now. That it's important to do the decent thing.'

'Do the decent thing?' he echoed.

'Despite what you seem to think, I haven't actually come here to have a go at you because you dumped me four years ago. People get dumped all the time. I'm just a statistic. I've grown up a lot since we were last together. And I certainly haven't come to beg you for one final fling! I'm here to tell you that you're a father.'

The silence stretched to breaking point. He was frowning, then he shook his head.

'Sorry but I think I may have misheard you.'

'No, Abe. You didn't mishear anything! I'm here to tell you that four years ago you fathered a child. Tilly is *your* daughter.'

'No! It's not possible...'

The instant the words were out of his mouth, he knew for certain he was wrong, that Georgie would never, ever lie about this. His stomach rolled and his

eyes shot to the photo that still sat on the table next
to him. Now that he looked closer, he could see that
Tilly was so very like him. Same dark hair and dark
eyes and smooth olive skin. She was utterly beautiful,
and his heart clenched. He swallowed uncomfortably.
Georgie must think him an utter fool for assuming
she'd taken up with another man the minute he'd left
and he'd been too distracted by his own jealousy to
put two and two together.

'The contraceptive pill I was taking failed when
I had that stomach bug,' she said flatly when it was
clear he was unable to convert his thoughts into
speech. 'Apparently that's not unusual. After you left
and I took a test, I stayed on at the hotel restaurant for
a while but there was no point hanging around, knowing that I was pregnant. I had to get back to England
and start sorting my life out.'

'I can't believe it's the first I'm hearing about
this...' Abe said unsteadily.

'I couldn't find you.'

'I... *Four years*... It's been four years...' He was
dismally aware he was rambling incoherently, but
couldn't seem to pull a sensible sentence together.

'You don't believe me that she's yours? Well, I said
what I came to say and to heck with whether you believe me or not!'

She flew towards the door, grabbing her jacket
en route, seemingly unaware that he was behind her,
his long strides eating up the space between them.

'You can't just tell me...*this*...and then try to run
away!'

Georgie spun around, her eyes filled with tumultuous emotion and resentment. 'Tilly is three years and three months old,' she said in a rush. 'You left a month shy of four years ago. Do the Maths, Abe. And if you still doubt what I'm saying then that's just fine with me! I'm not asking you for anything and I don't expect anything of you either. Believe me, I'm not *that* stupid. I just thought you should know and now you do, you can go back to your royal life...'

CHAPTER THREE

'WHERE DO YOU think you're going?'

He positioned himself directly in front of her and folded his arms. Six feet plus of immovable muscle.

'I'm going home. Where else would I be going?'

'Forget it.'

'Sorry?'

'No way are you going to run out on me without finishing this conversation!'

'What's there to finish? I've already explained what happened!'

'Don't be naive, Georgie.'

'Naive?' She laughed humourlessly. 'Believe me, if I was ever naive, that stopped the second I found out I was pregnant. Having a baby on your own makes a person grow up extremely fast, trust me. And if you knew me at all, you'd know that I would never lie to you about something like this.'

No. He already knew she wouldn't. As he stared down at her, Abe's mind was still reeling from a bombshell he hadn't seen coming. How could he be a *father*?

Fatherhood was obviously on the agenda, but at some vague future point in time. He had returned four years ago to the immediate stress of having to step up to the plate and take over where his father had been obliged to leave off and, since that time, he had given only passing thought to the inevitability of marrying and producing heirs, even though he had been pointedly introduced to several suitable women and even dated one, two years previously.

He'd refused to be rushed into anything. It would happen and it would happen at a time of his choosing and with a suitable woman, also of his choosing. But now? Fatherhood? A bolt from the blue hurled at him from nowhere and embedded into his rigorously controlled life without warning? He was struggling to take it in.

Abbas had grown up with the mantra of the importance of having a cool head when it came to the responsibilities of his position. He'd studied the history books and knew the history of his own bloodline all too well. He was well versed in how things could implode when emotion got the better of measured judgement—what his country needed was calm guidance. He'd watched, alone, from the sidelines as his father had fallen apart and then withdrawn at the death of his mother from cancer, and he'd decided as a small boy that falling in love was a road he'd never knowingly choose to travel. But the visceral emotion that had exploded inside him on discovering he had fathered a child with Georgie, a perfect little girl, suddenly warred with the cool, calm demeanour he'd spent a lifetime honing and the vision of practical duty he'd always pictured lay ahead of him. The impact of the collision felt as if it had just cracked something inside him, and he hurriedly sought to paper over it before it turned into a breach too wide to contemplate right now, when it was more important than ever that his country had the effective leader it needed. So that when duty finally beckoned, he would be fully prepared to control the outcome.

Except, as he eyed the mother of his child standing in front of him with a challenging tilt to her chin, it appeared that, far from being in control of any outcome, he was staring down the barrel of a gun, still clinging to the flimsy hope that somehow things were not as they seemed.

'You're in a state of shock,' Georgie stated as calmly as he wished he could sound right now.

'To put it mildly,' he said in a driven undertone.

'You want to believe that I'm making this all up but I'm not. I know you're probably wishing I'd kept my mouth shut because the last thing you need is… *this*…in your life, but I couldn't do that to you or to Tilly. It wouldn't have been right to keep the existence of your daughter from you. I know how important parenthood is. My father was there for me every step of the way after my mum died. I would never have dreamt of depriving you of at least knowing that you are a father, even if you choose not to do anything about it.'

'No, there is no way I would have rather you said nothing…'

He raked shaking fingers through his hair and stared at her, but he wasn't seeing *her*, he was seeing a future he hadn't predicted, frantically trying to re-calculate what this would mean for him and for his country. The ground was moving under his feet, as perilous as quicksand, but even so he meant what he said. She had come to say her piece and, even if she had blown a hole in his minutely planned future, he was still incredibly glad that she had told him. He already wanted to meet his new daughter with ev-erything that was in him. But on the heels of that thought came once again the sudden fear that the walls he'd fought for so long to build and reinforce were in danger of developing hairline cracks that he couldn't allow to worsen, which had him forcibly pulling himself together.

'You tell me that I have a child,' he said, his shoul-ders straight and his voice entirely steady now, 'and I believe you. But DNA proof will be required. Once we have that, then we can talk further.' He hesitated, cleared his throat. 'The photo. I would like to see it again.'

Georgie's eyes tangled with his for a few tense sec-onds then she looked away, rummaged in the bag to extract the photo and handed it to him and watched because this time he really *looked*. When at last his spectacular dark eyes lifted from intently studying Tilly's image and rested on her again, they were cool and unrevealing.

'Tomorrow,' he told her in a voice that left no room

for her to manoeuvre, 'I will arrange for a DNA test to be performed.'

'Don't you trust me to do it? No, don't answer that. Of course, you don't!'

'This has nothing to do with trust,' he countered quietly. 'Make sure you and…the child, Matilda, are available. I will personally text you to give you the details. Allow me to have your number.'

'Don't think you can order me around!' But her voice wavered because the implications of the situation were beginning to sink in. With the best of intentions she had clambered on board a roller coaster and she was only now realising that she had no idea how far it would go or how fast before she could get off.

But there was no reason why she shouldn't remain in full control during the ride, was there?

Whatever happened, whether he was royalty or not, she, as Tilly's mother, would always be in a position to call the shots.

'This is very far from ordering you around, Georgie. This is about a protocol that must be followed. I am a crown prince and a DNA test is not a matter of choice in this instance, but one of necessity. I hope you can see that.'

'Yes. I suppose so.'

The following day she kept Tilly home from nursery and fudged an excuse to skip work so that she could wait for Abe's doctor to make an appearance.

She had heard the ping of her phone at six in the morning and had read what she should expect and who.

There had been no sentimentality in the message, nothing to set her mind at ease. Practical information was imparted by Abe, and she was told that he would contact her at precisely nine that evening, by which time he would already be in possession of the results.

There was no choice given in the matter and it was hard to cling to the belief that she was in charge when she felt as though she were in the path of a steamroller.

When her cell phone buzzed next to her at nine sharp that evening, every muscle in her body froze.

The results are back. We need to talk.

Yes. Of course.

I will be over in half an hour.

What? Tonight?

Tell me where you live.

You can't rock up at nine in the evening!

Why? Is there someone with you?

No, but I have a child. Remember?

I think it's fair to say that it is a situation that needs to be urgently addressed. Your address?

Taut with consternation and aware of that steamroller gathering pace and moving ever faster in her direction, Georgie rattled off her address and then sprang into action.

Tilly was fast asleep, curled up under her duvet with just one foot poking out. For a few seconds, Georgie looked down at her daughter and marvelled at the absolute innocence. She drew the duvet over that tiny foot, smoothed down the rebellious dark curls and then quietly shut the door as she left the room.

She had only just managed to change into some old jeans and a jumper when her mobile rang and Abe announced his arrival.

Of course, there had been no doubt in her mind that he was Tilly's father but she was still a bag of nerves as she pulled open the door and fell back for him to brush past her.

She didn't have to see his face to sense his heightened, restless energy. It was there in the jerkiness of his powerful stride as he spun round on his heel to look at her as she closed the door to her flat quietly behind her and then pressed herself against it to stare back at him.

He dwarfed the small space. Her flat was tiny and she had gone for it because it had been in a good neighbourhood. Better somewhere small where she felt safe than bigger where walking through the streets with a small child posed a problem.

It was in a pleasant made-to-measure block overlooking the Thames with sufficient communal gardens to ensure her daughter had somewhere outside to play, because the trip to the nearest park was a bus ride away.

'I want to see my daughter,' he said abruptly, his lashes sweeping down to hide his expression.

'She's asleep.'

'I have no intention of waking her,' he pressed.

Georgie nodded. She unglued herself from the door and padded past him up the short, narrow flight of steps where two small bedrooms nestled on either side of a bathroom.

She stood aside in silence and watched as he tentatively approached the low bed and peered down in the semi-darkness.

What was going through his head?

Figuring it out was not beyond the wit of man, she thought. He'd been well and truly dumped in it and he was probably frantically trying to work out damage limitation.

'I'm sorry,' she told him stiffly, after ushering him into the kitchen and offering him something to drink.

Every nerve in her body was alive to his presence. Her back was to him but she was very much aware of him pulling out one of the kitchen chairs to sit. He had tossed his camel cashmere coat over one of the other chairs and when she finally turned to hand him the coffee she had made, she couldn't help but think how out of place that coat looked…how out of place *he* looked. Too expensive, too elegant, too sophisticated for her little kitchen where all the detritus left behind in the wake of an energetic toddler was piled here, there and everywhere.

With the width of the small white kitchen table between them, they could have been adversaries waiting for a fight to begin.

Regret at having told him what he evidently hadn't wanted to hear poured through her like poison battling against the certainty that she had done the right thing, for better or for worse.

Besides, how would it have played out if she had kept Tilly's existence to herself? What would have happened when the innocent toddler turned into an inquisitive adolescent who found out that she had been wilfully deprived of the opportunity to have a relationship with her own father?

Children didn't ask to be born. Yes, there were circumstances that dictated lives that were far from ideal, with absentee parents or parents who just didn't care, but she would never have been able to live with herself if she had made a unilateral decision to deny her daughter the chance of having two parents, even two who were no longer together.

'I wanted to tell you when I found out but couldn't…and when I saw you again, I'm sorry… I didn't think…' She stumbled over her words, shying away from the hard look in his dark eyes. 'You could have been married, for all I knew. Had kids of your own…'

'That would not have mattered,' Abe said evenly. 'The child sleeping in that bedroom would still have remained my responsibility.'

'I'm glad to hear that.' She extended an olive branch because a way forward had to be found, and if they were on opposing sides that was going to be impossible. 'I know a lot of men would find it easy to walk away from their responsibilities to a child they hadn't asked for. I know this might put you in a difficult situation…' She laughed uncertainly. 'It's not as though you're an ordinary guy and I know it'll probably be impossible for you to see much of Tilly, but I won't stand in the way if you happen to be in London and want to meet with her without being able to give me much notice.'

Every word hurt because never in a million years had she ever seen herself in this place, talking to the father of her child the way she would have spoken to a stranger. She had loved this man, given herself to him, *trusted* him and now what was left? The pain of disillusionment. Yes, she was happy that he wasn't going to walk away from Tilly, but it was a dagger through her heart to know that the only reason he was even sitting at this table opposite her was because he had no choice.

And, more than that…what happened now?

Losing both her parents had shown Georgie how desperately she longed for stability. Having Tilly had only reinforced those concerns and yet here she was teetering on the edge of the unknown and her hard-won stability felt as though it were disappearing like water down a plughole.

Trying to be detached, as he was, was the only way they would be able to deal with the situation in an adult, satisfactory manner but she felt sick from the effort.

'You're telling me that you will allow me to play a part in my daughter's life?'

'Well, yes,' Georgie said uncertainly. 'And, of course, if you want to contribute financially, then I won't stop you...'

'That's very generous of you,' Abe responded with just a touch of incredulity. 'I understand that for reasons beyond your control, beyond *our* control, I have been uninvolved in my child's life for the past three years, but I can assure you that the winds of change are beginning to blow.'

'What do you mean by that, exactly?'

'I mean that it is unacceptable for me to only play a walk-on part in Tilly's life. How do you imagine that would work? Realistically?'

'Well, I don't think there would be any need to get lawyers involved...'

'If you had been able to contact me when you found out you were pregnant, Georgie,' he said quietly, 'how do you imagine the scenario would have played out?'

Georgie thought that, had she been able to contact him, it would have entailed a whole series of alternatives that would have made things very different. It would have meant that he was still around or had at least given her his number, which would have implied that he would have wanted her to keep in touch…and that being the case, who knew? They might have actually remained together, had the committed relationship she had craved back then, given their child the best head start in life by being a *family*.

A sheltered upbringing had been her own worst enemy, had deprived her of the defences required to live life as he did—on an easy come, easy go basis before he married someone from the same background and elevated standing as him.

She had had a mighty learning curve since then. Reality left no room for romance and what she was facing now was reality. He was here and they would have to come to some kind of agreement about visiting rights.

'Like this,' she told him. 'Of course, I would have thought it would have been a bit more straightforward because I would have assumed you lived in the same country or else somewhere reasonably commutable, but I would have said what I'm saying now—that I would never stand in your way of seeing your child and would never stop you from helping out if that was what you wanted to do.'

'Participating in my child's life from a distance isn't going to work for me. I can't hop on a plane and visit every weekend and, even if I could do that, I wouldn't want to.'

'What are you trying to say?'

'Do you think it's fair for my daughter to be an occasional visitor to her father? To miss out on her heritage and birthright? Don't forget she's the first-born child of the Crown Prince of Qaram. She's en-titled to all the privileges that come with that. Would you deny her access to the very best of everything?'

Georgie gasped at the implication that Tilly had in any way been disadvantaged. 'How *dare* you? I have worked hard every single day to give Tilly the very best I could! You have no idea what it felt like to return to London, single and pregnant, with all my dreams put on hold, terrified that I wouldn't be able to earn a living!' Shaking at his insinuation that what she had to offer Tilly was paltry in comparison to him, Georgie sprang to her feet and stalked across to the sink, putting some space between them while she gathered herself.

She stood staring out of the window by the kitchen sink, her back to him, hands braced against the coun-ter and taking deep breaths because, right now, she could have hit him.

She froze when she felt the weight of his hands on her shoulders. She turned around slowly, caged in and suffocatingly conscious of his proximity.

Her eyes flickered to the hard lines of his face then dropped to his wide, sensuous mouth and skit-tered away before her imagination could start fill-ing in blanks.

'Georgie, that is not at all what I meant to imply. You've done brilliantly under very difficult circum-stances,' he said stiffly.

She folded her arms and reluctantly raised her eyes to his face. 'How else could I take it? This may not be up to your standards,' she said tightly, 'but it is *my* castle and I have never stopped counting my lucky stars that I had the means to buy it so that there was at least a roof over our heads when we needed it.' He'd dropped his hands but he was still so close to her that she could feel the warmth of his breath on her face. 'I was alone and afraid, so don't you *dare* swan in here and say you could give her more than I have! She's loved, and she knows it, and that means a lot more than material possessions, even solid gold ones!'

Every single word was a proclamation of how much he had hurt her with his thoughtless words, and Abe knew that her bitterness would be the greatest impediment to what could be the one and only conclusion to this bombshell situation.

There was no choice going forward for either of them but marriage. Anything else was unthinkable. He could not conceivably have a child and commute a handful of times a year to pay lip service to visiting rights. He hadn't asked for a child, but he now had one and there was no part of him that did not intend to be a hands-on father.

But this was not exactly a straightforward situation.

Not only was there the matter of breaking the news to his father and, in ever-increasing circles, everyone else in his country, but there was the even more significant challenge of trying to persuade a woman who clearly hated him that they had to get married.

He would have to be at his most persuasive. He

would have to put his natural inclination to get what he wanted, whatever the cost, on hold. In fact, he would have to dispense with that line of attack completely. He had already taken legal advice on what his rights were and, despite his prominence, wealth and royal status, the rights of a mother who had taken on the role of single parent for over three years won hands down in any court of law. Not only had she been the sole provider for Tilly in his absence, but she had tried to find him at the time of her pregnancy and it had been entirely his fault that she had found that an impossible task.

He could, of course, point out the considerable advantages to marrying him—not least a lifestyle of such breathtaking comfort and downright opulence that she would never want for anything in her life again—but he had an uneasy suspicion after what she'd just said to him regarding material possessions that, as persuasive arguments went, she might not be as bowled over by that one as another woman might be.

She had tried to contact him three years ago and yet there had been no financial motivation behind that as she hadn't known who he was, and it would seem there was no financial impetus behind her contacting him now.

How did that make sense?

'Can I ask you something?' he murmured, watching her with veiled eyes. He propped his hands against the counter on either side of her, his dark gaze wedded to her attractively flushed face.

In this moment, he was entirely taken with the strength of his own response to her, bemused by the peculiar hold she still seemed to exert over him. Once upon a time, it had seduced him into staying in Ibiza for far longer than necessary and now…

'You obviously have a problem with me.'

'Do you blame me?' she asked.

'That's a question that could keep us going round in circles for ever. You have a problem with me and yet that didn't stop you from doing what you felt was the right thing to do.'

'Why would it?' Georgie said defiantly.

'Because, and this is just my cynicism winning the argument, a woman with an axe to grind against a guy she thinks unceremoniously dumped her without an explanation could do one of several things…'

Georgie wanted to break free from that devastating gaze but she was spellbound by him, locked into immobility and barely able to breathe.

'What things?' she asked, as the drag on her senses grew more powerful by the second.

'She might decide to have no further contact with him, whatever the circumstances. Alternatively, she might make contact with the aim of using the child as a pawn in a game of payback. More likely, however, a woman might be tempted to see what was in it for her financially, especially when she realises that she's dealing with a man who has the wherewithal to change the direction of her whole life. Yet you fit none of those categories.'

'This is so…hard for you, isn't it?'

'What do you mean?'

Georgie looked down and blinked rapidly. She folded her arms and stared at her feet, jutting in between his legs.

He pushed himself away from her and on impulse reached for her hand and twined his fingers through hers.

He led her to the sitting room and she followed, and she didn't resist when he gently sat her down on the sofa and positioned himself next to her.

'Talk to me,' he urged as he tried to find some solid ground, however small.

'We don't even know one another,' Georgie said honestly. His fingers were still entwined with hers and she was reluctant to break the physical contact because that physical contact felt good, like a lifebelt in stormy seas. She looked at him, searching for the right words. 'Okay, so we once had a brief fling. But you weren't who I thought you were, and in a way I was pretending to be a different person as well.'

'Explain.' He frowned.

'I'd had a very sheltered life, raised deep in the country. I went to the local village school and then to the local secondary school. The most exciting things to happen were the school dances and a trip to the cinema. It was always my dad and I and it was an easy life with none of the temptations, I guess, that I would have had growing up in the city. Going to university was the first time I really took in what life outside a small hamlet in the middle of nowhere felt like.'

'Frightening?'

'Exciting.' She could feel some of the tension oozing out of her. 'An adventure for a rural girl like me.' She blushed. 'I… You asked how it is that I wanted you to know about the pregnancy even after I found out that you'd dumped me without a forwarding address.'

Abe tilted his head to one side and waited.

'My dad…my dad was the local vicar, Abe.' She laughed self-consciously. 'I never considered not doing what I felt was the right thing to do. You can fight against a lot of things, but you can't fight against your upbringing and, as you can imagine, I was raised with a great many moral codes firmly in place.' She could feel her cheeks stinging with colour. She suddenly realised he was as guided by his own rigid upbringing as she was and she softened slightly.

'A vicar—'

'I didn't tell you,' she rushed in hurriedly, 'because I knew that it would put you off sleeping with me. You'd be surprised how many guys are put off the minute they hear that. When I went to Ibiza, I guess I felt I needed to try and be a different person. University had prepared me for the big bad world out there, but, for the first time, I no longer had my dad to back me up and I suppose I wanted to do something out of my comfort zone. Taking a gap year…working at that hotel…dealing with an everyday life that wasn't planned out…it was all new to me. I was frightened and alone and desperate for *new* to distract me from what I'd been through, what I was *still* going through.'

* * *

'A vicar…' Abe murmured a second time, almost as shocked by that admission as he had been by the bombshell baby news.

And now many things slotted into place—from her shy charm, which had bewitched him, to her conviction that he should know about his daughter, without any hidden agenda aside from the fact that she was 'doing the right thing'.

And then several other considerations fell into place and by far the one outweighing all others was his recognition of just how devastated and abandoned she would have felt when he'd left. She would not have had the usual armour in place that many women of her age might have had. She hadn't taken any knocks in her life before, and then he had come along and unwittingly delivered a whole series of them…and just after she'd lost her beloved father.

Guilt and shame that he'd been the cause of even more hurt twisted his insides and he almost couldn't bear it when she continued.

'So I just can't believe that I'm in this place, with a child from a guy who didn't want me, who doesn't know who I am.' She shook her head. 'At any rate, I've managed very well for the past three years, whatever you may think.'

What Abe thought was that never had he felt so badly positioned on the back foot or so determined to make things right for both Georgie and Tilly.

'You make a very good point,' he acknowledged, mind now firmly made up on the only way forward that he could see for the time being. 'We *don't* know one another, but that doesn't detract from the reality that we share a daughter and, as someone guided by having to do the right thing, wouldn't you agree that the right thing would be for us to remedy that oversight as quickly as possible?'

Georgie shot him a dubious look from under her lashes. 'Of course, we will have to be on speaking terms…' she agreed.

Abe swept aside her interruption to continue, levelly, reasonably…but determinedly. 'Tilly has a heritage that she has every right to know, a grandfather who would be overjoyed to meet her, a country which she should, I'm sure you would agree, get to know as it is, at least in part, *her* country too…'

'Yes…well…'

'*Our* duty, Georgie, is to make that possible, wouldn't you agree?' He left the question dangling persuasively between them, challenging the moral codes she lived by, demanding the one and only response she could give.

The sort of half-in, half-out relationship she envisaged for them wasn't going to work but he knew full well that breaking that news to her right here and now wouldn't be wise. He had hurt her badly, and it was time to put things right in the only way he knew how. He was positive Georgie was already an excellent mother, and he wanted to prove both to her and to himself that he could be just as good a father to Tilly. In fact, the increasing drive to do so kept sending shockwaves deep inside him, and he was forced to keep a tight rein on his self-control. Becoming emotional had never worked well for anyone, particularly his father, and he utterly refused to go down that road himself. It only led one way, to certain loss and pain.

'So the first thing we need to do,' he murmured, 'is to start by getting to know one another much better.'

'You mean…we become friends? After everything that's happened between us? I think that might be asking a lot but I'm willing to keep the channels of communication open.'

'Tilly is only three. Would you be prepared to let her see my country, without you there as chaperone?' He made an expansive gesture with his hands that implied the prospect of that was just fine with him.

'Tilly wouldn't go anywhere without me,' Georgie said, sounding alarmed at the disturbing picture being painted of her daughter ferried out of the country to be surrounded by strangers who spoke a different language.

'Nor should she. So perhaps you would like to hear what I propose?' He ignored her scepticism and carried on soothingly, placatingly…the very voice of reason. 'I suggest you *both* come to Qaram with me, then. It is urgent that I return and, rather than rushing my first contact with my daughter here, on borrowed time, I will be able to devote time and space to getting to know her in Qaram. We need to work on this as a unit if we are to do what's best for her, as parents. So…are you in agreement?'

He found himself holding his breath, waiting for

her response. Everything in him was urging him to make her his wife, but for once, he would have to be satisfied with settling for this small step forward.

CHAPTER FOUR

How could Georgie argue with the calm logic of a guy who wanted to do what was right? She couldn't. So she would go.

She hated to leave Duncan in the lurch and wondered what she should say about taking a chunk of time away. Should she come clean and explain the situation to him? That was an option she dismissed as fast as it raised its head. Why would she do that? Whatever the outcome of the talks she and Abe might have, she would end up back in London and would want to continue with her career at the hotel, irrespective of what financial arrangements were made regarding Tilly. She and Tilly were two separate entities and she was smart enough to realise that, while he would feel duty-bound to support his daughter, he certainly had no obligation to support a woman he had walked away from, whatever justification he might feel he had had for doing so. Nor did she have any intention of trying to squeeze any money out of him for herself.

* * *

Yet money would have to be something to be discussed because that was the world he lived in.

They were different people with different dreams, different goals, different *standards*. If there was some ridiculous, lingering physical attraction towards him, then it could be explained away easily enough by the fact that he was her first lover and, as things had turned out, her last. He'd shown up out of the blue and, of course, nostalgia had swept aside the years and deposited her right back to that place where she had only had eyes for him. She hadn't had any experiences with anyone else and so could not call upon a present to help eradicate the past.

She would visit his country because it made sense to do so but she would maintain distance between them, would discuss future arrangements in a businesslike fashion.

He had asked if he could look at Tilly once again as she had slept and had remained standing by the side of the low bed for a lot longer than Georgie had expected, gazing at his daughter intently, almost as though he could will her awake, then he had finally left, having given her a million and one instructions as to what would happen next.

The trip. What to expect. What she should bring with them. How she would get there. The driver… the flight…

She had agreed to meet him in Qaram and so it was something of a surprise when she opened her door the following evening to see him standing outside, minus bodyguards and casually dressed in a pair of jeans and a jumper with his coat hooked over one shoulder.

'Why are you here?'

Acutely conscious of the fact that she was in her pyjamas even though the clock had yet to strike nine, she remained defensively by the door, before relenting and letting him in with a sigh.

'There is something I feel we should discuss before you come to Qaram.' He turned to look at her for a few seconds and she thought she caught a flash of wariness and uncertainty in his eyes, before his magnificent lashes swept down to conceal his expression. When he lifted them his gaze was cool and steady once more, and she decided she must have been mistaken. 'I contemplated waiting until you were there, when things might have been a little less rushed, but, on reflection, I think this is something I really need to say to you before you come...' He shrugged, suddenly looking uncomfortable, and her gaze sharpened. Perhaps she hadn't been mistaken after all.

'What is it? Why are you looking so serious?'

'Let's go and sit down.'

'You're worrying me, Abe.'

He smiled reassuringly. 'Don't be worried.' But he waited until they were sitting facing one another in her small sitting room before leaning forward, forearms resting lightly on his thighs. 'I had hoped that my beautiful country might help me build my case for what I am about to say, but then I decided that not being on home ground might put you in an awkward position...'

'I have no idea what you're talking about, Abe.'

'Yesterday, we discussed…' he hesitated, his eyes keenly on her puzzled face '…in a manner of speaking, a possible way forward for us.'

'Yes, because you want to have a role in Tilly's life, don't you?'

'And yet I am a prince.'

'I haven't forgotten, Abe. How could I?'

He sighed and shifted in his seat. 'I haven't even met her properly yet, but already I know that it will never be enough for me to simply dabble in my daughter's life.'

'What are you trying to say?'

'I would like you to marry me, Georgie. I genuinely believe this is the best way ahead for us.'

Georgie's brain sluggishly absorbed what he had said but refused to break it down into bite-sized pieces. She stared at him, confounded, until he asked gruffly, 'Did it never occur to you it might be an option?'

'Marry you? *Marry you?*' She stared at him wordlessly. No, she could say with her hand on her heart that she hadn't seen this coming. If Tilly had been *his* bolt from the blue, then this totally unexpected proposal was *hers*.

To show up at this hour for a conversation like this? With their leaving for Qaram a matter of a heartbeat away? How on earth could he expect her to agree to *marry* him?

'You need to think about it,' he said, rising fluidly to his feet.

'You're *leaving*?'

'I will see you again in a couple of days.'

'You can't just drop this on me and then walk away!'

'Is that a direct quote from me?' he teased.

Georgie glared at him and he returned her look steadily.

'Yes, that's exactly what I intend to do, Georgie. Leave you to think about this with no pressure. Come to Qaram. Experience what life over there is like and keep an open mind. Remember—if my life is about to change, then yours is about to as well…'

He couldn't have done a better job of sending her into a tailspin.

She spent the next two days feverishly playing and replaying that marriage proposal in her mind. Had she seen it coming? No! But he was right, she should have. How could she have possibly thought that a crown prince wedded to the notion of duty would be happy to accept the role of part-time dad to his own flesh and blood living on the other side of the world?

It didn't help that he refused to discuss it on the three occasions when he had telephoned her.

'When you get here,' he had told her, gently but very, very firmly, 'then we can talk about it. There's still a lot of water under the bridge between us, hence the importance of having plenty of time to consider my proposal.'

Georgie had refrained from asking what would happen if and when she refused. She didn't want to confront that issue over the telephone either. He'd been shrewd enough to have left her mulling over his explosive proposition knowing that she would have to gnash her teeth and wait until they were face to face to discuss the ramifications.

She didn't think anything could stop the ceaseless churning in her head, not even Tilly's excited antics at the thrilling change to her routine, but the shock of being ushered like royalty into a private jet certainly did the trick.

She had been wrenched out of her comfort zone, every atom of self-control and self-preservation hijacked by the astonishing change to every single thing she had ever experienced in her life before.

Tilly was cheerful, inquisitive and blissfully accepting of the deference accorded them. Once in the private jet, which was so luxurious that Georgie had to make an effort to keep her mouth shut lest it hit the ground, she had proceeded to explore every nook and cranny not out of bounds. She blithely babbled away non-stop to the crew, which included two minders and a charming young girl who seemed to have a never-ending array of tasty finger food, which kept appearing at various intervals.

By the time the plane began its descent, Georgie was exhausted and Tilly was asleep. She gasped as the heavy door slid open and the heat assailed her.

Looking around her for some familiar point of reference, her eyes fell on the sleek black limo slowly heading towards the jet.

Abe. It had to be. Relief washed over her as she

made her way down the metal steps with Tilly draped over her, softly snoring.

From behind the blacked-out windows of his chauffeur driven limousine, Abe watched Georgie as she emerged from the jet, pink-faced and bemused, with Tilly in her arms.

A sudden wave of protectiveness threatened to overwhelm him. In the space of a week, he had rediscovered a woman he'd never forgotten and become a father to a child he was yet to meet while she was awake!

A beautiful daughter. A woman who would become his wife, if he could just convince her to see things his way. That this was right. That this made perfect sense. A marriage of convenience between two consenting adults, both of whom would put Tilly at the forefront of their lives. He wouldn't make the same mistake as his father by falling in love with his wife, devastating him and their child when she died. No, he would go into this marriage with his eyes wide open, as would Georgie, and, with no expectations of love on the table, nobody would get hurt. It was the ideal solution and he would strive with everything that was in him to bring it about.

He vaulted out of the car before his driver could obey protocol and open the door for him, and walked towards Georgie.

She was in a pair of trousers and a blouse and she looked utterly at sea.

'Abe!'

Abe paused as Tilly, still nestled into Georgie's shoulder, opened her eyes and looked at him drowsily for the first time.

His daughter...his flesh and blood...

He had felt more than a twinge of guilt knowing that the proposal he had left Georgie to mull over could only really have one outcome. Because Tilly was his heir, a princess in her own right. She would need the protection only he could provide. He just had to find the right way to explain that to Georgie.

He had already explained the situation to his father, who assumed that they would be married.

Any guilt, however, was swept aside the minute he saw Tilly. He reached out, displaying a lot more confidence than he felt, to take her from Georgie, so he could hold her for the very first time.

She was warm and soft against him and he breathed her in, astonished at how primal his urge to protect her was. Where his defences were used to being up when it came to the entire human race, this small child had managed to obliterate them simply by being his daughter.

'How was the flight over?' he asked, ushering Georgie into the blissful cool of the limo, relinquishing Tilly to her as she slid in.

'Very smooth, thank you.'

'You must feel out of your depth, but please don't.' He sat back, angling himself so that he could look at her. She looked flustered and uncomfortable. 'It might feel very alien for a while being over here and I'm very grateful that you agreed to come. It was a big step and an important one for Tilly to be introduced to Qaram.'

'Not that she'll have the faintest idea what it's all about.'

'She's here and I'm here and we will have to explain who I am to her.'

'She's too young to ask questions or understand the answers properly,' Georgie said truthfully. After the bewildering and hasty preparations to get here, she felt drained and there was still so much to discuss. His marriage proposal seemed like a dream, but it wasn't. It was just that she couldn't face talking about it now, when it could only lead to an argument she wanted to avoid on day one. Defences down, exhausted as Tilly sleepily nuzzled against her shoulder, she rested against the seat and closed her eyes. Abe was here, an anchor in this alien environment whether she liked it or not.

'Growing up in the vicarage…' she half yawned, not opening her eyes '… I had loads of contact with young children, especially in challenging circumstances. Parishioners would come, pour out their problems, brings their kids with them and I would play with them, look after them, talk to them. They're very robust. Much more adaptable than adults think they are.' She turned to look at him and blushed at the intensity of his dark gaze. Outside, an arid scenery flashed past but then the sprawl of the city began taking over and her interest was piqued.

She asked questions, sat straighter. There was a

minimalist beauty about it. Tall white buildings, glass and steel, as modern as anything to be found anywhere.

'There aren't many people walking around,' she remarked, turning to him.

'You live in London,' Abe said wryly. 'You're accustomed to pavements thronging with people. My entire country has a fraction of the number of people living in London alone and yet it is much bigger. You will never see crowds surging along roads. The intense heat also makes it uncomfortable to be outside for long periods of time.'

'I like that,' Georgie admitted. 'I went to London after Ibiza because that was where I knew the jobs would be. One of the guys at the restaurant I worked at was related to Duncan. He recommended me for the job. There would have been nothing for me in the country but I missed the peace and the quiet.'

'Was it…hectic caring for a young baby amidst the chaos of an overpopulated city?' Abe asked.

'Exhausting. You try taking an infant on public transport. Nightmare.'

Abe felt another stab of remorse that she'd gone through that experience all alone, without him. If he'd been there for her when Tilly was a baby, they'd have been married by now… He made suitably empathetic noises and spent the rest of the trip explaining just how calm Qaram was, how still the dunes were at night, how clear the skies were. The subject of his marriage proposal sat like a white elephant between them, but he knew this was neither the time nor the place to bring it up and he guessed she felt the same. In the temporary lull, he intended to push the advantages of his country as much as he could. All was fair in love and war, even if it was paternal love he was fighting for…

'You could almost count the stars,' he said lazily, noting the way her eyes automatically travelled up to the clear violet skies above them from which stars were appearing as obliging gold studs against deepest purple velvet.

'Sometimes,' he murmured, his voice purposefully seductively soft, 'in the desert, if you listen hard enough, you can hear the movement of the sand. It is like a whisper.'

He knew the heat and the newness of the surroundings were massive points in his favour and before the discussion about his proposal began in earnest he wanted her to think beyond her obvious objections to see a much bigger picture. He really wanted her to agree of her own accord without feeling backed into a corner.

His sprawling staff were waiting for their arrival, primed to expect a companion and her young daughter. If they suspected anything, they were well versed in remaining silent and were all so utterly loyal to him that gossip would have been unheard of. At any rate, they would all discover, in due course, that he would be getting married to her, that she was the mother of his child and a woman with whom he had fallen in love but had been forced to leave until Fate decided to throw them together once again. A story of exceptional romance that would capture the hearts of his entire country, not just his staff. He wouldn't allow a whiff of scandal to be attached to Georgie or Tilly, so for them he'd bear with the image of a man in love.

'Wow.'

Darkness had shielded the splendour of the palace, but it was unmistakable the second they stepped foot through the door. White and marble dominated an entrance hall big enough to host a ball.

'I'll show you to your quarters,' Abe murmured, dismissing the congregated staff with a near invisible gesture. 'You look dead on your feet.'

Georgie nodded, too tired to pay much attention to her surroundings but awed by what she saw as he scooped Tilly from her and headed up one of two impressive staircases.

'Where are our bags? I can't believe you live here…'

'I'm a prince. What did you expect?' But there was amusement in his voice.

'I didn't really give it much thought.'

'Your bags will be delivered to your suite.'

He pushed open a door and stepped aside and Georgie walked into an antechamber that led to a central living area off which were two bedrooms separated by a bathroom. All this she took in in a single sweeping glance.

'My bedroom adjoins yours,' he told her, 'and there's a connecting door. There will be two nannies available day and night. From tomorrow, they will be entirely at your service and would be offended should you choose not to avail yourself of their services.'

'I'm not used to…all this…' Georgie whispered, shorn of her fighting spirit for once. She looked at him anxiously as he channelled her towards the smaller of the bedrooms. Tilly was too sleepy to explore but Georgie could see an array of toys in a wicker basket and everything she might need for a toddler.

She was happy to sit and watch as he slid off his shoes and squatted down to his daughter's level, interacting a little awkwardly, glancing to Georgie often for approval, but he wasn't shying away from the attempt and he was trying hard to connect.

He would have given instructions about the bedroom, she thought, would have predicted that a young child might be wooed with toys and so he had imported them. The soft linen was also child friendly. He'd had just a couple of days but in that time he had obviously given a lot of thought to how a three-year-old toddler might be made to feel comfortable away from the only environment she had ever known.

He'd been *thoughtful* and Georgie sleepily welcomed that.

After fifteen minutes she could hardly keep her eyes open and Tilly had been popped into her pyjamas and climbed into her bed, clutching the stuffed rabbit she had brought with her, her eyes fluttering closed.

'I'll take you to your room,' Abe said and before Georgie could object he had lifted her off her feet and was carrying her through to the second, much larger bedroom.

Georgie wound her hands round his neck and leant against him and closed her eyes. It was delicious being in his arms again, and almost a shame when he gently deposited her on the enormous four-poster bed with its lavish coverings.

She watched him as he went to close the heavy drapes and then he strolled towards the bed and perched on the side.

In semi darkness, with just the light outside filtering through the door, which he had left ajar, he was all shadows and angles and she shivered.

She sat up and drew her knees up and gazed at him.

'We still need to talk,' she whispered. 'When you left, you said that—'

'It's late and I can see you're very tired. Maybe we should talk about it tomorrow?'

'I can't get it out of my head. You asked me to *marry* you, Abe.' She looked at him with feverish urgency, but he was right. She was exhausted and on uncertain footing and this was a conversation definitely best left for when she wasn't dead on her feet. 'You shouldn't have left me to think about it.' She stifled another yawn.

'It was important that you had time to consider what I put in front of you, Georgie. Responding in the heat of the moment would not have been a good idea. If I could have stayed longer in London, we would have had the conversation there, but I had to return to Qaram, hence…' He shrugged.

'I suppose so.'

'Don't think about that right now.' He lowered his eyes, his ridiculous lashes once again shielding his expression, but when he raised them to look at her, there was genuine sincerity in his gaze. 'I cannot imagine what life must have been like for you, coping with a pregnancy on your own, and then a tiny baby on your own. Having to settle Tilly into a nursery so that you could join the workforce and earn a living to put a roof over both your heads and food on the table…' He shook his head, clenched his fists and breathed in deeply. 'It must have been so hard.'

'It was.'

'But you are here now,' he said in a low voice. 'I want you to seize this opportunity to relax and allow yourself to be looked after. Your every need will be unhesitatingly met.'

Having conjured up the memory of how it had felt to struggle on her own and how wrenching it had been to leave Tilly in a nursery when she was only a baby, Georgie found that every word from his mouth tasted like manna from heaven. His voice was calm and soothing and she sighed in pleasure.

'I have arranged for us to have dinner with my father tomorrow evening. He is keen to meet you both.'

Georgie nodded drowsily.

'You don't have to be apprehensive,' he said, correctly sensing her hesitation. 'He…he hasn't been the same since his heart attack but for the first time I saw real pleasure on his face when I broke the news to him about Tilly...'

He feathered her cheek with his finger and she breathed in sharply and closed her eyes. She knew that this would pass, that she was feeling vulnerable and out of her depth and yet...never had she wanted anything more in her life than to touch him. He'd hurt her so much when he'd walked away and had hurt her again when she'd seen him again and realised just how fleeting a reference point she'd been in his life. Not even much of a footnote.

Yet right here and right now, she felt safe with him. How was that possible? She could remember every touch, the feel of his body and the way he'd made *her* body feel. She shut the door on those thoughts but she could feel them pressing to get out.

'Your father,' she whispered, 'I know you say that he's looking forward to meeting us and that he's over-joyed, but he must be disappointed that you've ended up in this situation.'

'I see that you've decided that an in-depth conversation trumps going to sleep.'

He grinned and Georgie smiled back at him. For a moment he was shorn of the aura of power that made him seem so formidable. For a moment, he was the same guy she had fallen for four years ago.

'Well, it feels weird being here, Abe. I've never known anything like this in my life before. A week ago, I was taking public transport to get to work and spending weekends with Tilly at the park, and now...

I'm in a palace with nannies round every corner and sitting on a bed that's as big as my entire flat.'

'Bit of an exaggeration there.'

'I wasn't prepared for something like this.'

'Sometimes, life throws you curve balls.'

'This is more than just a curve ball, Abe.' She sighed. 'Your father would have expected you to marry someone who was raised for this sort of life-style.'

'You need to stop worrying about that.'

'Easier said than done.' She looked at him. 'I wish you'd be honest with me. This can't truly be what you wanted for yourself. Me and Tilly on your doorstep...'

'I think she's going to enjoy being here.' He could feel the conversation drifting into territory best avoided right now, especially when her eyes were closing and sleep was taking over. She was nervous and out of her depth and he wanted to reassure her but it was a delicate balancing act.

Fear of the unknown was driving her towards a maudlin interpretation of what she could expect here. He put himself in her position, tried to imagine what it must have been like for her when she found out that she was pregnant.

He tallied the image with his memory of the girl he had left behind, the one who, as he now knew, had just lost her father and been left all alone in the world.

When he'd met her, she'd been shy, hesitant to start any kind of relationship with him. That, in itself, had been a pleasing novelty. With or without his regal status, Abe had never had trouble when it came to attracting women. Any women. All of them. The feeling of having to work to seduce a woman was a concept as alien to him as commandeering a rocket and flying to the moon.

So when she had politely turned down his offer for dinner, he had been intrigued but he had never thought that something begun so casually would end up consuming his interest with such power.

He'd been there to buy a hotel. Serious business for someone intent, not only on eventually running the country when his father retired, but investing in businesses that could bring recognition to Qaram and provide additional wealth to help his people.

Staying with just one bodyguard at one of the most expensive hotels on the island had meant there had been no shortage of women interested in finding out more about him. Having a bodyguard in tow was always guaranteed to engender lots of attention from the opposite sex and he had turned a blind eye to every curious glance slanted in his direction.

Craving a bit of normality, he had ditched the bodyguard for one evening and sauntered into the town to breathe in an atmosphere that wasn't as suffocatingly rarefied as the one where he had been staying.

And there she had been, working in a restaurant.

She had emerged flushed and blushing from the kitchen, anxiously awaiting his verdict on her food and braced for something disparaging. He had seen it written on her face.

And when he had complimented her, she had lowered her eyes and smiled and it had made him feel ten feet tall.

He'd immediately asked her out. Of course he had! He hadn't been going to be hanging around for long and he'd been consumed with an urgent need to see her, to go out with her, to sleep with her.

She'd refused but he hadn't given up and neither had he regretted the pursuit, because he had enjoyed her company more than he could have imagined possible.

She'd…enchanted him.

He hadn't known about her father. When he thought about that now, he could remember that there were times when he had surprised her wearing a lost expression on her face and times when there had been a hyper quality to her that had seemed at odds with her reserved nature.

Then he flashed forward to him leaving, and then to imagining her discovering that she was pregnant.

When he thought about that, something inside him twisted and he suddenly found it hard to swallow. An imagination he'd never known he had fired up with a series of graphic images, heartbreaking images of her searching for him, gradually coming to terms with the reality of his disappearance.

He had been called away, yes. Events had galvanised him into returning to Qaram and that in itself had been a frightening time for him. He had really and truly thought that he had done the right thing walking away from a situation that could never have developed into anything permanent and he'd already been navigating a very fine line delaying his departure more than once to remain in her bed. He'd never done that before for any woman, but he'd repeatedly pushed that thought away at the time. He genuinely hadn't known just how emotionally vulnerable she had been because she hadn't told him about her father's death. Would he have pursued her in the first place, slept with her, if he'd known?

Abe had a sinking feeling he'd have been drawn to her regardless, but it was a moot point anyway.

The fact of the matter was that she was here now and those winds of change he had mentioned were about to blow her ordered world to pieces.

'But you can't really think about that at the moment, can you?' he murmured understandingly, and she stared at him in silence. 'You've been wrenched out of what you have spent the past four years building and now you feel you've lost your foothold.'

'It's…'

'I know. Scary.' He half smiled and glanced around at the magnificent bedroom that made her seem small and wide-eyed and lost all of a sudden.

This was where he'd grown up. He barely noticed the opulence of his surroundings any more. He was accustomed to living in a palace, where rooms flowed into other rooms, where there was so much space that the problem was what to do with it all.

And, yes, had he had an arranged marriage, he would have found a wife whose background would have fully prepared her for this lifestyle. She would have moved in exalted circles, would be acquainted with all the unspoken mores and traditions and customs that would have been expected of her.

No wonder Georgie was at a complete loss.

'And you don't want scary, do you?' he asked pensively. 'You want stability.'

'More than anything in the world,' she breathed with heartfelt sincerity. 'I lost my mother when I was young, but life grew around that loss, like skin growing around an open wound until it scars over and stops hurting so much. When my dad died, my whole world fell apart. Now that I have Tilly, I want to make sure that she has all the stability in her life that I haven't had…'

Abe privately thought that she was making an extremely good case for marrying him, but that was a point he wasn't going to make just yet.

'I understand.' He looked to the door. 'You should try and get some sleep now. Is there anything you need? Food? My private plane is usually well stocked but if there's anything you want…'

'I'm okay.'

'Still nervous about meeting my father?' He smiled, reassuring her, wanting her to have a good night's sleep as free of worry as possible given the circumstances.

It was important she didn't see this as an ordeal. It was also important that he establish a footing between them in which conversation could be had without the past overshadowing everything.

'Where does he live?'

'Would you be alarmed if I told you that he, too, lives in a palace?'

'I would be surprised if he didn't.' She smiled.

'It's smaller than this one, though.'

'I guess it couldn't be any bigger. What on earth do you do with all these rooms, Abe?'

'They're occasionally filled with diplomats, members of state, visiting dignitaries...' He laughed, his dark eyes drifting to her mouth. She had a perfect mouth. He could remember exactly how it had tasted and he wanted to kiss it again now. His pulse picked up a gear and he shifted uncomfortably.

This pull of intense attraction felt even stronger than those recollections of the many times they had spent together in her bed. He was uneasily aware that what was supposed to have been a brief fling had never really felt like that to him, but it had taken meeting her again to really bring that point home. He tensed, but then reminded himself that not everyone shared such an intense physical connection. Yes, that was all it was, amazing sexual chemistry. There was no question of it being anything else. At that thought, his tense muscles relaxed.

'Weren't you ever...lonely?' Georgie asked, interrupting his unwelcome thoughts.

'Lonely?' Abe opened his mouth to deny the suggestion, his long-standing habit of politely knocking back anyone daring enough to try and venture into his private life, but instead he heard himself say, thoughtfully, 'I guess...maybe there was a point in time…' He laughed but when their eyes met, hers were sympathetic.

She didn't say anything and for once he wasn't the one using silence as a means of extracting information.

'When my mother died,' he admitted, 'I was also young. My father took her death extremely badly. He carried on ruling the country, he talked and walked and performed his duties as he always had, but unfortunately I was the one who saw behind that façade and it was tough for a child. In truth, I lost both my parents that day. My mother through death and my father through many months of mourning.' He shook his head, surprised at the direction of the conversation. 'By the time he surfaced, I had grown up.' He slapped his hands on his thighs, ending his astonishing deviation from the straight and narrow. 'Right, then, should there be anything at all you need…' he nodded to a buzzer by the side of the bed '…buzz and someone will bring whatever you request.

She reached out and her slim fingers lightly curved over his wrist.

'I'm really sorry, Abe. Yes, you must have been very lonely indeed.'

They had moved closer to one another. How had that happened? The atmosphere was suddenly heavy with feeling and with a powerful, invisible bond that took them away from the charged present back to the past they had shared.

She trembled and her eyelids fluttered as he traced his finger along her cheek.

Of course, he was going to kiss her.

She *felt* it with every nerve in her body and she *wanted* it with every nerve in her body.

She sighed, mouth parting, her whole body straining towards him. In her head, she had yearned for this so much and so many times but now, as his lips found hers, she realised that no imaginings had come close to replicating the fierce sizzle of electricity that zapped through her.

His tongue invaded her mouth, meshing against hers as he drove her back against the pillow.

His fingers weaved through her short hair and the heavy weight of him against her reminded her of hot, sultry nights when they'd done nothing but make love for hour after hour.

He suddenly drew back with a shudder and vaulted to his feet and, in turn, she squirrelled back up into a sitting position, aghast at her loss of self-control and hating herself for having succumbed to the treacherous demands of her body, seduced by the fact that he had talked to her, really talked to her, for the first time that she could remember.

She wasn't here playing tourist! And she certainly wasn't here as his lover!

She was here to discuss a life-changing future and she was utterly dismayed at how fast she had lost track of that.

She couldn't look at him, but she could feel his eyes boring into her as he moved to stand by the door, looking over his shoulder with one hand on the doorknob.

'Don't forget,' he said evenly, 'we meet with my father tomorrow for dinner.'

'I won't.' Her voice was as controlled as his, thank goodness.

She only realised that she'd been holding her breath when the door clicked quietly shut behind him, and she exhaled long and slow before flopping back onto the pillows and staring up at the ceiling.

CHAPTER FIVE

GEORGIE AWOKE TO sharp brightness pouring through
a slit in the thick curtains in her bedroom.

It took her a few moments to orient herself and to
work out where she was, in a strange bed in a strange
house in a strange country... No, in a strange bed in
a *palace* in a strange country!

She was in pyjamas and she took a few mental
steps backwards to remember the events of the day
before.

She'd left one world behind and stepped into a completely different one, like stepping into that magi-
cal wardrobe and being transported to a mythical
kingdom.

In all her confusion, Abe had been the one constant
and she had clung to him. She knew that Tilly had
taken everything in her stride and adjusted with en-
viable ease to their exalted surroundings before flopping into bed in the adjoining bedroom in their suite.

While she...

She groaned and buried her head in her arms because recall of that searing kiss the night before leapt out at her, gleefully reminding her that of all the stupid, *stupid* things she could have done, passionately kissing Abe had to be right up there.

She'd kissed him and she'd *wanted more*. She'd been dragged back at speed to where they had been four years previously and every single memory had risen to the surface, firing her up and setting her body alight.

Her response had been a heady combination of buried lust and a surge of dependency on him because he was the only thing in this strange new world that seemed to make any sense.

She had no idea how she'd managed to make her way to the bathroom and actually have a shower and change into pyjamas before collapsing into bed, but she had and now...

New day, new way.

She leapt out of bed, flew into Tilly's bedroom and then all hell broke loose when she realised that her daughter was missing.

She spent five minutes hunting her down, opening and closing cupboards, panic levels rising by the second, before she remembered the all-important buzzer by the bed whereby anyone could be summoned at any time of the day or night.

She summoned.

Within minutes there was a knock on her door and she yanked it open to Abe standing in the doorway with Tilly in his arms and Georgie's first instinct was to pull her daughter away from him and hold her tight.

Tilly responded by vehemently protesting while Georgie glared at a composed and cool-as-a-cucumber Abe.

'What the *heck* is going on?' She tried to keep her voice controlled for the sake of her daughter, who was demanding release, but she was shaking with anger.

'Nothing is *going on*,' Abe responded, looking slightly taken aback by her frantic response. 'Mind if I come in?'

'Yes!'

'Mummy, I want to *play*!'

'Play *where*, Tilly?' Georgie was finding it impossible to contain a wriggling toddler and, with a sigh of pure, teary-eyed frustration, she stepped back, allowing Abe to brush past her before swinging around and pinning her to the spot with his dark gaze.

Georgie fell back. Their eyes met and hers involuntarily dipped to his sensuous mouth, hot colour staining her cheeks as she remembered that kiss of the evening before.

'What's going on, Abe? Why wasn't I called when Tilly woke up?' she demanded in a more restrained voice.

'I thought that you might sleep a little more soundly than you expected and in a new environment, Tilly might not necessarily wander into your bedroom, not knowing the layout of the suite, so I positioned one of my people by the door to the suite and to inform me immediately if there were any signs of a small, curious child on a mission to explore.'

'I should have taken her into bed with me. I planned to but I was so tired.'

She deposited Tilly on the ground and hugged her arms around herself, awash with guilt.

'Go get changed,' Abe said gently. 'I will take care of Tilly while you do.'

'You had no right,' Georgie muttered helplessly, watching as her daughter wandered off back towards her bedroom and the familiarity of the handful of soft toys that had made the journey with them. Through the open door, Georgie could see her happily holding bunny by the ears while sourcing a few more from the suitcase on the ground.

'I am her father.' Abe's voice was reasonable. 'You may not want to accept it yet, but I have every right.'

'She doesn't know you.'

'She knows me a lot better now that I have had a chance to spend some time with her. Go and change, Georgie, and try to stop seeing me as the bad guy in all of this, because we'll never get anywhere otherwise.'

She was still in her pyjamas. Her pyjamas consisted of an old tee shirt with a cartoon character on the front and a pair of stretchy sleeping shorts that left very little to the imagination and she was suddenly conscious of how little she was wearing.

Hard on the heels of that came a surge of heat and she nodded abruptly. 'Okay, but we need to talk.'

'Yes,' he agreed. 'We most certainly do. We will be seeing my father later, and before then we have some important issues to iron out. I have made sure that Tilly has eaten. When you're changed, I will take you to where Tilly has just been playing—supervised, I should add, by two highly qualified nannies, just in case you might be tempted to think that I might be witless enough to not provide the necessary safeguards for my daughter.'

'I didn't think any such thing. Don't put words into my mouth, Abe.'

Important issues to iron out…

Georgie knew exactly what he was talking about. That marriage proposal. It had been put on ice because he had wanted to give her time to digest what he had put on the table but now there was a thread of steel in his voice and she quailed at what lay ahead of her, a complete unknown.

She had spent the past few years struggling to make sure her life was as secure and as stable as possible, that *their* lives, hers and Tilly's, were as secure and as stable as possible. It was all she had wanted. For Tilly to have stability. She knew how disorienting and painful a lack of security could be. Now all of that was up in the air and she felt sick at the thought of how she could try and correct it.

She had a sudden, fierce longing for the routine of her poorly paid hotel job and for her small flat and those trips to the park on rainy weekends.

It might not have been grand, but that life had been *hers*, and now she was scared stiff because it had been ripped out from under her feet.

She hurried off to change, casting one last look at

Tilly, who was happily introducing Abe to her stuffed toy collection.

She would need to remember that, whatever his position and whoever he was, he didn't get to have the last word on their daughter. She was Tilly's mother and she had been a damn good parent for the past three years, so she was sure her rights would always trump his in any court of law.

She dressed in a pair of cut-off jeans and a tee shirt and wished she'd thought a bit harder about the sort of clothing that might have been appropriate to wear in a palace, but then she shrugged and decided that she didn't care.

They both looked up as she returned to the huge sitting area, Tilly with a broad smile and Abe smiling as well but his dark eyes rather more guarded.

'Are you playing tea party, Tills?' Georgie ignored the towering alpha male lounging on the ground next to his daughter, his long, muscular legs stretched out in front of him, his body language loose and relaxed.

She could feel his eyes on her, though, as she stooped down and ruffled her daughter's hair.

She was so smooth and soft, her baby skin pale gold and her eyes as dramatic and dark as her father's. When she smiled, there were dimples in her cheeks and she was smiling now.

'Mummy, there's a toy shop here.'

'Is there, baby? Where?'

'I'll show you.'

Georgie looked at Abe, who flushed and looked ever so slightly uncomfortable.

He uncoiled his long body and gracefully stood up, reaching out to tug Georgie to her feet and releasing her as soon as she was standing next to him.

A moment of physical contact quickly withdrawn.

'Well?' she asked as they headed down a marbled corridor wide enough to house sitting areas on either side. Impressive chandeliers interrupted the fresco painting that snaked along the ceiling.

'Perhaps,' Abe said as Tilly skipped along ahead, pausing now and again to make sure she was on the right track and that they were right behind her, 'I should first tell you the sequence of events for today?'

Georgie tensed. 'I know. We need to talk about the whole marriage thing you threw at me before you returned to Qaram.'

Abe winced.

One step forward, two back, he thought with an internal sigh.

Every word she had just spoken indicated that this was not going to be anywhere near as straightforward as he'd hoped. Ha! Who was he kidding? He'd known it was never going to be anything like straightforward persuading this woman to marry him. She really was like no other he'd ever met. He tried to gather his patience, knowing that if he wanted to bring this to a successful outcome, to ensure his child would be safe with both parents to support her, he would have to tread extremely gently.

But he couldn't help feeling it was a frustrating setback after what had felt like a pivotal conversation the day before. He'd thought that they had connected, but now he could feel the tension radiating from her in waves.

Would there ever be an end to her fighting him? To him, it felt as if their marriage was inevitable, but he was clearly dealing with a one-of-a-kind woman who was blind to all the material advantages that would be gained that way.

'We will leave Tilly with Fatima, one of her very enthusiastic nannies.'

'And does she know who Tilly really is?'

'I expect she has made an educated guess,' Abe said wryly. 'Of course, she will breathe nothing of her thoughts until an official announcement is made.'

'Of course not,' Georgie muttered.

Casting a sideways look at her, Abe smiled. He'd always appreciated the way she'd spoken her mind, gentle as she was, and, despite his frustration with her stubbornness, he was glad to see that the years had done nothing to alter that trait. It showed her spirit was just as strong as it had always been.

She could be truthful with him that he was a father because she had a keen sense of what was right and decent, and yet she could argue with him till the cows came home about a marriage proposal that, from his point of view, was as right and as decent as her admission had been. He *almost* rolled his eyes…

'We will have brunch together in the sun room. I have issued instructions. We can then discuss…'

Georgie straightened and stared directly ahead.

Tilly had disappeared through one of the doors. 'The Proposal,' she filled in for him.

'Indeed,' Abe said with a smile. He could practically hear the capital letters.

They were at the entrance to yet another massive space and Georgie stared, mouth dropping open, because when Tilly had said there was a *toy shop* in the palace, she hadn't been kidding.

'What's this?' she asked faintly, turning to Abe, who was slightly behind her.

Ahead the space was dominated by a soft play area worthy of any commercial venture. To one side was a small village comprised of several houses, varying styles and all big enough for Tilly to play in, and outside one of them was a ride-on miniature Mercedes Benz with its own electric charging point. There was a craft area with an assortment of crayons and paper and a sketch pad mounted on an easel.

'I had no idea what toddlers enjoy…er…playing with…'

'So you decided to get *everything*?' she squeaked.

'Actually, I had to restrain myself,' Abe admitted guiltily and was gratified when she burst out laughing.

'I should be really mad,' Georgie teased him, while behind her Tilly was busy picking up where she had apparently left off, under the supervision of a smiling girl who was sitting on a small kids' chair by one of the toy houses that were almost big enough to hold an adult.

'You surely cannot have much more annoyance left in your reservoirs,' Abe teased back.

She blushed like a teenager. Always had. He'd always found it irresistible. She was a glorious rosy colour now and his eyes drifted inexorably to her parted mouth.

He hadn't meant to kiss her the evening before, but it had felt so natural, and, once his mouth had hit hers, rational thought had disappeared through the window.

He had shot back in time to when he hadn't been able to see her without wanting to rip her clothes off.

He considered what marriage had always meant to him, something he had always assumed would be a formal and possibly sterile arrangement, a union forged for the sake of a country.

He thought now, as he stared hard at her full mouth and did his best to resist the urge to run his finger along that bottom lip, that marriage to Georgie would definitely have its upsides. He might not be able to fully give himself to her emotionally in the way she'd prefer but he would certainly be more than prepared to give himself physically to her just as often as she wanted.

He lowered his eyes and gathered himself.

She might hate him for what he had done, resent him for the position he had put her in, but he had kissed her just once and all that hatred and all those resentments had faded away under the seething passion that still burned between them.

Georgie felt the charge suddenly running between them, a chemical reaction she didn't seem capable of preventing, and she turned away sharply to focus on her daughter and then, for the next half an hour, to get to know the young girl who would be helping look after Tilly, because there was no doubt in Georgie's mind that she would need a bit of help while she was here.

Tilly was energetic and curious, and Georgie had no idea how she could help her daughter explore and run around when she was unfamiliar with the layout of the palace.

Nerves kicked in once again when Abe, who had remained in the room for the entire time, stood up and said something very quickly to the nanny in his native language before turning back to her and indicating the door.

Would Tilly burst out crying? Georgie wondered.

Left alone with someone she had only just met? But attending nursery from a very young age had, by necessity, turned her into a sociable child and there were no tears as the door to the playroom was very gently shut behind them.

Phase three was about to begin, she thought as she followed him wordlessly down another bewildering route. Same marble, different grand paintings and mosaics and balustrades but presumably a different destination.

Phase one had been the introduction of the idea of marriage, which had been followed by phase two, the introduction to his country and the life she and Tilly could have here, and now phase three was about to commence and she realised that, in the tumult of everything that had been happening, she hadn't thought enough about his proposal to consider possibly up-rooting herself from everything she had ever known.

It had lain there, on the periphery of her mind, a bridge waiting to be crossed.

The room into which she was ushered was lavish. She could understand why it was called the sun room, because a bank of arched glass doors allowed brilliant light to wash in, diluted by clever use of shutters and very fine muslin panels. It overlooked gardens she hadn't noticed before and beyond that, as she moved to gaze through one of the windows whose shutters had been flung open, she could see the rise and fall of sandy dunes.

The marble here was black and white on the floor and the furniture was white wicker intermingled with upholstered sofas and on a sideboard was a veritable feast.

Her chef's eye appreciated the effort that had gone into its preparation.

They helped themselves to food, the silence stretching between them until she could feel her skin break out in a thin film of nervous perspiration.

'You have had some time to think now, Georgie.' He sat down and dumped his plate in front of him and watched her as she sat opposite him at the glass table.

'But it's all been such a rush…'

'I have stepped back from discussing my propo-sition,' he said, ignoring her lame excuse, 'because I thought you might want time to think about it. I also wanted time to adjust to parenthood and the reality of having a child. To launch into the nitty-gritty of a marriage proposal seemed…too hasty.'

'Abe.' Georgie sighed helplessly. 'I believe in marriage. I just don't believe in *this* marriage. I really want you to be a huge part of Tilly's life and I know you've said that you can't possibly be a part-time dad, but surely where there's a will, there's a way?'

'Why?' Nothing in his voice betrayed any emotion other than mild curiosity at her answer.

'Because I always thought I'd be married, and married for the right reasons, married for love. I'm as traditional as you are, Abe, but I do recognise that this is the twenty-first century and people no longer feel that they have to shackle themselves to one another because they happen to have had an unplanned baby together.' She looked around her, at the opulence. 'I know I can't provide this level of material comfort for Tilly but there's more to life than that.'

'I agree that money isn't everything, but that's being incredibly simplistic about our situation,' Abe told her quietly, his eyes suddenly intent on hers. 'You told me about Tilly because you felt I had a right to know. Now, you want me to believe that you have our daughter in mind when you out of hand reject my offer of marriage. Are you sure you are not only thinking of yourself?'

'That's not at all what I'm saying,' Georgie protested heatedly. She leant towards him, her slight body trembling with tension. 'I'm saying that marriage without love would be a disaster and you don't love me.'

He closed his eyes and when he opened them she could have cried at the bleakness in them. 'And you say this in the full knowledge that every marriage that starts with declarations of love ends up with living happily ever after?'

'No, of course not...'

'Because there are no guarantees, even if love is involved, are there, Georgie? If my memory serves me right, you told me yourself of the many hours you spent with the children of divorced parents...' Whether parents chose to separate, or it was forced on them through death, the true victims of love, he considered, were always the children. Love hadn't given either his or Georgie's parents a happy ever after, only grief for the remaining adult and child. Perhaps, if coming together to start a family was approached in a more logical way, as he was proposing, there would be fewer casualties along the way?

'Which is just what I don't want for Tilly!' she declared.

'And I repeat, you imagine that love will be a guarantee against that? It won't. Listen to me, Georgie. I have no intention of being a part-time father. I wouldn't want that if I were Joe Bloggs from the house next door and I certainly cannot and *will not* accept any such arrangement given my position. Tilly is a princess in her own right, will be wealthy in her own right, even if you refused to marry me, and she will need qualified protection as she grows up. Can you provide her with that?'

Driven onto the back foot by questions she hadn't

even considered, Georgie scrambled to make a case for herself but there was a trickle of doubt in her mind. Surely she wasn't being selfish in wanting love to be a part of the equation? But could love trump Tilly's safety? She shivered at the thought.

'Tilly also has a heritage here that is centuries old and it is one she deserves to know. Not to be *acquainted with* but to *know*. Would you willingly deprive her of that too, Georgie? In your quest to find love?' he asked with a raised eyebrow.

'It's not a crime for me to want a life with someone who loves me,' she protested in a whisper.

'No, of course it isn't. But in this case, surely you agree that your *wants* cannot take precedence over the *needs* of a child too young to make decisions for herself? I want my daughter to grow up *here*, to inherit what she is due, to be safe while she is doing so, and to have the best possible upbringing. Will you stand in the way of that because you crave a fairy-tale life that largely doesn't exist?'

Assailed by doubts on all sides, Georgie blanched. How could the life she wanted, which was one she had been brought up to expect, suddenly seem like a self-serving dream only attainable at the expense of the most important person in her life?

Her heart was thudding. Would she be willing to sacrifice Tilly's future for her own?

'There is no point in going round the houses,' he said, voice flat. 'Tilly deserves the best that life has to offer her and, more than anything else, that means being here and having the unity of both her parents at hand for her. Together. Married. And the business of love has nothing to do with it!'

Georgie marvelled that he could wipe out something as important as that with a dismissive slash of his hand, but then, as she had just discovered, he was nothing like the warm, passionate man she'd once known. Now, he was a man as cold as the Arctic waters when it came to emotions.

And she had fallen for him. She, with her belief in love and her casual acceptance that her life would follow the same path as her parents', a loving union that stayed the test of time.

She had fallen for him and she hadn't managed to clamber out of the hole she had dug for herself four years ago because she still had feelings for him, even though everything inside her railed against the injustice of that. Wasn't that why she was so conflicted over marrying him? He made her hope and made her yearn for the impossible and she hated him for that. Every second with him was a reminder of the perils of still having feelings for him when he had none for her.

'I will do everything within my power to do what I think is right for my daughter and, by extension, for you,' Abe said quietly, almost sympathetically, 'but, as a matter of interest, can I ask how you would feel if you got your own way on this?'

'Sorry?' She rubbed her temple with her finger, tiny circular motions to relieve the tension.

'Here is another scenario for you, Georgie. In pursuit of an impossible dream, you return to London. Tell me how you would feel when Tilly is old enough to understand that in *your* best interests, you decided to deny her the sort of life she could have had here, and how would you feel when she *does* come over here to be with me and whoever I may marry in the future, a woman who will have a say over how Tilly fills her time, what she does, a woman who will doubtless bond with her and with whom I will make joint decisions about things we choose to do as a family? How will that play out with you? What if, at that point, you still have not found Mr Right? What if, when you wave goodbye to Tilly, you return to life on your own knowing that our daughter will be absorbed in family life on this side of the ocean? What if, by walking away from my proposal, you discover that the very stability you want Tilly to enjoy ends up with me and a new family here, rather than with you over there?'

Georgie stared at him in consternation, for he could have said nothing more destructive to her peace of mind.

She waded through the imagery in her head and surfaced to acknowledge one thing, and that was, however damaging he might be to *her*, his number one concern was, without doubt, for his daughter. Everything he had said was out of consideration for Tilly. She had overturned the direction of his life in the most devastating way possible, but he had not turned away or tried to fob her off with money to buy her silence. He openly wanted to admit Tilly as the legitimate heir to his kingdom, to marry her, Georgie, even though that meant sacrificing the more normal route he would have wanted to take to find his bride.

In other words, he had not baulked at self-sacrifice.

And now that he'd asked, how *would* she feel if he married someone else? *When* he married? Because of course he would. There would be no angst-ridden questions about finding the right woman. He would interview some suitable candidates and choose someone fitting for the role of wife to a prince and he would make it work. Emotions wouldn't be involved and, with a child to consider, the imperative of a wife would be pressing. He was right, while *she* looked for Mr Right, he would simply move on with his life and by Tilly's next birthday would probably be wed and ready for the next phase in his life.

'I don't want to have to fight you,' he said softly.

'What does that mean?'

'I will fight for full custody of my daughter, if needs be.'

'I'm her mother!' But Georgie's blood ran cold. Yes, she knew her rights, but could those rights be undermined by the extraordinary circumstances of their situation? Could he hold the trump card just because he was a prince? And was that something she wanted to risk?

'I would never aim to exclude you from our daughter's life, Georgie, but likewise I would never roll over and give up the fight if you decided to return with her to London.' He sat forward and looked at her urgently. 'I don't want a war on my hands and the truth is that, tradition or not, I would not find it palatable to force you kicking and screaming into a marriage if I thought the whole edifice would collapse in due course…'

'What are you saying?'

'We got along four years ago, Georgie, and we get along now. Drop your weapons and you might find that we rub along very well together.'

She wondered what would happen if she dropped all her weapons and forgave him for the past. What would she open herself up to? For him, putting the past behind them would herald a pleasant future rubbing along nicely. He'd always assumed he would have an arranged marriage and, in the context of an arranged marriage, 'rubbing along nicely' would be deemed a successful outcome.

For *her*, though…putting the past behind her might open up an even bigger Pandora's box than the one already open. How long before the creeping love that had never gone away staged a comeback, as they 'rubbed along nicely' in their marriage of convenience?

That thought frightened her. Could she live a life on shaky ground when all she'd ever aimed for was security? Or had she already gone past that point by entering this royal world?

'I don't even like you, Abe, after what you did…' But her voice was not quite as steady as it should have been and she was frowning, unable to look at him.

'You sound as though you have become so accustomed to thinking like that, that you're finding it hard to let the sentiment go, but you have to try, for Tilly's sake.'

Georgie blinked and focused on him.

She was spellbound by his beauty. He sat there, so coolly confident in every word that left his mouth, and his very confidence was making a mockery of her concerns.

'This isn't my world,' she protested weakly and he waited a couple of seconds before replying.

'If you become my wife, my world will be yours, as it will be our daughter's.' He paused and this time his dark eyes were lazy and speculative and sent a trail of fire coursing through her.

She fidgeted and realised that somewhere along the line she had closed the distance between them.

Suddenly hot and restless, she sprang to her feet and walked jerkily across to the window to stare out at this world he promised would be hers. Behind her lay a fabulous brunch, barely touched, and a fabulous room, furnished with all the regal pomp money could buy. Ahead of her lay splendid grounds and the vast panorama of desert beyond.

She was unaware of Abe approaching her from behind although she suddenly saw his reflection in the floor-to-ceiling glass through which she had been staring. Her heart stopped and then accelerated. She turned around and he was so close to her that if she reached out and placed her hand on his chest, she would feel the beating of his heart.

'Marry me, Georgie,' he said, voice low, dark eyes searching her face. 'Get past your resentments so we can make it work.' He reached to place his flattened palm on the glass behind her, caging her in, eyes intense and mesmerising.

'I am not the enemy…' He paused and his eyes roved over her face. 'In fact, I am very far from that, as that kiss last night demonstrated…'

'That was a mistake.'

'Was it? Truthfully?' he asked huskily.

She knew that he was going to kiss her, and she *knew* that that kiss would throw everything into turmoil…because she was going to respond. Her body was melting and she knew he was right. She couldn't pretend that she didn't find him as compelling now as she had four years ago.

Still, she shivered as his warm lips touched hers and then groaned as his tongue traced the contour of her mouth before delving in to taste her. She clutched at his cotton shirt and tugged him closer so that his thighs were hard against her and nudging between her legs and, oh, it felt *so good*.

He was the first to break apart, but he stayed close, staring down at her upturned face, rosy with passion.

'We don't just get along,' he murmured, 'we have this going for us too, and it is far more than just a bonus…'

CHAPTER SIX

THE SILKY SOFTNESS of his words washed over her, as seductive as an embrace.

What had she thought might happen when she had decided to tell him about Tilly? Not this.

And yet, if she backtracked to that very first moment when she had seen him standing in that room, with his back to her, bodyguards by the door, a tall, dominant figure, a prince…the process of working out just where everything would lead should have begun.

She'd told him that she'd said goodbye to naiveté the minute she'd found out that she was pregnant. You had to wise up very fast, as a single mother, to cope with the demands of parenthood without any support and particularly without the support of the father because he'd done a runner, vanished without a forwarding address.

So what if he was a prince? she had thought when they'd been unexpectedly reunited. She would do what she had to do, do the right and decent thing, and if he wanted some kind of contact with his child going forward, then she would be happy to accommodate him.

On every count, she had completely misjudged the situation.

Had she really thought that she would have emotionally recovered from the devastating effect he had had on her? He'd been in her head pretty much every day for four years. That in itself should have been a vital clue telling her that he was still dangerous when it came to her emotions, yet she had turned a blind eye to that peril and bought into the illusion that she would be able to handle whatever was thrown at her. She had thought that it would be easy because at the end of the day, as Tilly's mother, she would always have the last word.

But Abbas Hussein was a crown prince, which made having the last word a great deal trickier. He was a man of honour and duty and those qualities had come to the fore in his unhesitating response to the situation he had faced.

Surprising? Maybe not. He might have walked away from her all those years ago—and she could almost, *almost* follow his logic in doing that—but the truth was that she would never have fallen in love with someone who *wasn't* decent and honourable.

And that decent and honourable man wanted, of course, to do the decent and honourable thing.

Like finding herself in a maze, she could now look over her shoulder and see that every step she took would inevitably lead her to where she was now even though she'd imagined herself to be completely lost during the journey.

He'd laid out his reasons for marriage with a level-headed logic that characterised this new Abe that she was starting to get to know. He'd shown her, in small steps, just how willing he was to involve himself in Tilly's life, to incorporate her into his magnificent royal world, even though he had never asked for her to be born.

He had been thoughtful and patient in his handling of the situation, even if Georgie suspected that he had known from the very start where things would end up.

And of course the one thing she hadn't anticipated, but should have, had happened.

She had fallen in love with him all over again and with love came hope and that was something that had no place in her situation.

And now this...

The chemistry between them, a kiss that had sent her soaring into orbit and the knowledge that, although he might not love her, he still wanted her.

Marry him, a voice whispered inside her, *and you'll do what's right for Tilly... Marry him and you won't have to live your life watching from the side-lines as he moves on with someone else... Marry Abe and you can have him in bed with you at night, wake up with him in the morning...*

He was right, they did get along, when she wasn't busy remembering how much she hated him, and she knew that she only hated him because of what he did to her, what he made her feel for him, and not because he was a hateful person. He wasn't. His very response to what she had thrown at him was testimony to that.

'Well?' he prompted, stroking her cheek with one finger and making it impossible for her to think straight. 'Respect…trust…and mutual physical attraction. It's enough for a successful marriage, enough to give our daughter the life she needs and deserves, don't you think?'

'I c-can't think when you're looking at me like that,' Georgie stuttered with utter sincerity, and he laughed just as he used to.

'Good. Maybe I don't want you to think. Maybe I just want you to agree with every word I say.'

'That's the most arrogant thing anyone could ever say!' She gasped but he was still laughing, still looking down at her in a way that was making her blood boil, and she lowered her eyes and smiled reluctantly.

'I suppose it makes sense,' she told him. 'I never thought I would marry someone because it makes sense, but this does.'

I'm marrying him because it makes sense but also because I love him, Georgie thought suddenly.

He would never know that, it was a pointless love that would never be returned, but she knew that if she really hated him there was no way she could ever accept his proposal, regardless of his arguments.

'Could I have something a little less lacking in caveats?' he teased, further lowering her defences.

Georgie looked at him, eyes clear. 'Well, then, yes. I accept your marriage proposal.'

She paused and he cupped his ear with his hand, frowning.

'Why are you doing that?'

'I'm waiting for the *but…*' He smiled, eyes lazy. 'And I am very glad there appear to be none. You're doing the right thing. Give this a chance and I promise you will find in me a husband who will not let either you or Tilly down.'

He curved his hand along the nape of her neck and then smoothed it over her shoulder.

Desire bloomed inside her in a sudden, shocking burst. It was as though, in accepting his proposal, she had mentally freed herself from the business of denying her attraction to him.

He must have sensed that because he drew just a tiny bit closer, his breathing quickened and there was a slumberous look to his eyes as they rested on her flushed face.

'Come upstairs,' he urged, and Georgie made a feeble attempt to tell him not to be crazy.

'I have to go and see how Tilly is doing,' she said, but she didn't pull away as he continued to stroke the side of her neck, his touch so soft and gentle that she almost moaned aloud.

'Of course, you must, if you feel you have to,' he agreed.

But the floodgates had been opened and she didn't want to shut them.

She was going to marry this man and there was no way she could expect the marriage to remain a celibate one. Not only would that have not been feasible, neither of them would have wanted it.

There was a real and tangible pull between them, and deep inside her she felt that was something, *hoped* that it was something that had stuck with him as it had stuck with her.

Excitement flared.

Marriage! So the circumstances didn't quite live up to her girlish fantasies of the perfect situation but, as she had discovered from experience, nothing in life was perfect and as solutions went this was a good one.

'But I think you'll find Tilly is fine,' he murmured. 'Fatima has me on speed dial. If there is a problem, then I will know within seconds. I also have a camera installed so that we can check on her at any time if we feel the need. Fatima knows it's there, indeed was the one to suggest it, so…'

'Your father…what time…?'

'I will perhaps take Tilly over slightly ahead of you, which will give him time to get to know her. I plan on leaving here in…' he glanced at his Rolex '…a couple of hours and my driver will be on standby to deliver you to his palace at six-thirty this evening. It's going to be an informal affair.' He smiled faintly. 'So we have a couple of hours to play with,' he said wickedly. 'Would you like to play with me, Georgie?'

Georgie blushed furiously. She had made love to this man so many times and had had a child with him and yet, as he looked at her now, she felt like a virgin on her wedding night to the man of her dreams, shy and tentative and yet fizzing with excitement.

'Dare to walk away from old resentments,' he challenged. 'I know you want me. I want you too. And we are to be married…' He smiled and she felt faint and in thrall as he took her hand and they headed upstairs, headed to his bedroom suite, which adjoined hers.

She made a point of peeping in to check on Tilly as they went past the playroom. She wasn't going to rush into bed with him just because he snapped his fingers! Her heart was beating with nervous anticipation but she wanted him so badly. The genie had been let out of the bottle and was running amok and there was no way she could think of shoving him back in.

She felt his presence looming behind her as he lounged indolently against the doorframe while she coddled Tilly and hugged her before the siren call of the playroom beckoned the little girl back, then she turned and looked at Abe, drowning in his dark, inviting gaze.

There was acquiescence as she twined her fingers into his and he squeezed her hand in response.

The atmosphere was thick with anticipation and she half expected him to hurry her to his bedroom, intent on following through but, in fact, he took his time as they headed up the imposing staircase and when he opened the door to his suite, he seemed in no rush to do anything.

He stood back as she walked into a space that must have been twice the size of hers and certainly bigger than her entire flat in London—far bigger.

'By royal command,' she said, catching his eye, and he grinned.

'Command is not a word I associate with you.'

'I'm here, aren't I?'

'Royal consent, shall we say…?' He strolled towards her and then reached for her hands, holding them lightly as he looked down at her. 'That is what this marriage will be about, Georgie,' he said seriously. 'Never command, always consent. I know you feel that you may have been coerced into this position, primed to wear my ring on your finger when you hadn't envisaged that being the outcome when you first decided to tell me about Tilly, but we're both on new territory and we have to consider that our actions from now on will have our daughter as the centrepiece of whatever we decide to do. Agreed?'

Georgie nodded, but couldn't help her heart twisting a little. She would always want to put Tilly first, but wondered if there would ever be a place for her, Georgie, in his reckoning. It would be best not to hope for that, she decided. It would hurt too much when inevitably it didn't happen. So she would focus on making Tilly happy instead.

'And I think you'll agree,' Abe continued huskily, tugging her gently towards him, 'that happy parents are parents who physically enjoy one another…'

Georgie looked at him with wry amusement. 'Really, Abe? I don't think I've ever heard that definition before…'

'You should have.' He looped his hands behind her and then lowered his head and kissed her, long and slow, leaving her trembling for more. 'Don't they say that people who play together, stay together?' he muttered against her lips.

'I think they may have meant racquetball and golf.' She was laughing now, relaxed as she hadn't been since he had walked back into her life.

'Then that is a serious omission on their part.' He led her through the outer sitting room, which she belatedly appreciated was more personal than the other areas of the palace she had seen. Perhaps he had had a hand in choosing what sort of décor he wanted and had decided to lose the acres of clinical pale marble in favour of the warmer tones of wood, or maybe it was the fact that the silk rugs breaking up the space were more colourful.

Likewise, the paintings on the wall were less austere. There was a clutch of lined drawings that looked very Picasso-like and a couple of abstracts that brimmed with vigour and colour.

And beyond, lay his bedroom.

Her nerves fluttered but she was fired with anticipation. She'd dreamt of him for so many long months and even when the dreams had stopped, he'd always been right there, on the edges of her mind, a constant thought in her head.

She was led into a bedroom dominated by a super-king-sized bed with a velvet headboard that matched the drapes that pooled on the ground. The sun poured through the windows and he moved to shut the curtains, plunging the bedroom into cool darkness.

Abruptly sheathed in shadow, Georgie felt a sharp tingle of intense excitement. Her eyes adjusted to the darkness after the brilliance of the sunshine outside and she caught her breath as he moved towards her, undressing slowly as he did so.

Like yesterday, she remembered the first time she had slept with him, the nerves, the racing, pulsing thrill, the warmth of feeling that she was safe with this man.

Against all odds, she felt the same now.

He was already half naked and Georgie stared in open-mouthed fascination at the ripple of muscle and sinew. He had the perfect shape, broad shoulders tapering to a washboard-hard stomach, and just the right amount of dark hair across his chest. He was all male, oozing dangerous sexuality, and he was *all hers…*

For reasons that were right or wrong.

How had she made it onto the bed?

She didn't know. She must have sidled onto it as he'd strolled towards the window to draw the curtains.

At any rate, she was kneeling on the bed now, hands on her thighs, barely breathing as trousers followed in the footsteps of the shirt, falling onto the floor, leaving him in silky boxers and the prominent bulge announcing that he was as turned on by her as she was by him.

She followed his progress towards her and arched up to meet a kiss that was surprisingly gentle, a simple tasting of one another. She drew her hand softly along his cheek, contouring it and losing herself in the feel of his skin against her fingers.

'You realise,' he murmured, clasping her fingers in

his hand and looking at her, 'that we're turning over a new page, and there will be no going back now.'

'What do you mean?'

'My bed becomes *our* bed. We'll get married, Georgie, and I sincerely hope you'll be able to say goodbye to resentments so that together we can begin the process of smoothing over old scars. No more fighting, no more trips down memory lane, no more recriminations. I think we should focus on the present rather than the past, and look towards the future, as a family. We might not be the kind of family you've always imagined, but it will be ours, whatever we make of it.'

He would do his utmost to make both his wife and daughter happy, and he knew the best way he could make Georgie happy was to remind her exactly how good they were in bed. He might not believe in romantic love, but he definitely believed in the powerful chemistry between them. He would make this as easy for her as he could. He remembered his own vast pain when his mother had died, when his father had emotionally vanished, leaving him lost, alone. It had taught him the importance of self-reliance, of containing that which could cause hurt. Love. He would never allow Georgie to step into a place where she could end up hurt because of this marriage, or him, and so he would remind her of what they'd once had between them, and that would be enough for both of them...

'I get that.'

Of course, he was right.

She would have to come to terms with a new page being turned over and if, as he'd said, it didn't resemble the page she had hoped for growing up, then it could have been a whole lot worse.

He'd very graphically painted a worst-case scenario already for her. The one that involved him moving on with his life, absorbing Tilly into it, while she watched from the outside like the little matchstick girl peering through the window to a banquet she couldn't enjoy.

Oh, yes, that was definitely a worst-case scenario for someone who couldn't envisage anyone ever taking her place in her daughter's life.

They got along and they were certainly attracted to one another. Both those things counted for a lot.

She was smiling as he joined her on the bed, smiling as she pulled him down to her to nuzzle the side of his face and luxuriate in the feel of him against her.

'It's been such a long time.' She sighed.

'Long enough for me to want to take my time,' Abe responded unevenly, 'but also long enough for me to suspect that that won't be happening. Take your clothes off, Georgie. I want to see your nakedness. I want to see the body that bore our child.'

Abe had no idea how he was managing to have anything approaching a conversation because his body was on the verge of exploding. How long had he wanted this? She'd just said that it had been a long time. She had no idea how long it felt as he sat back and watched her peel her top off, revealing small breasts pushing against a simple cotton bra.

He dimly wondered whether a secret yearning for just this moment had been inside him for four years.

Not possible, surely!

But it felt like it as he watched her as she shifted off the bed, elfin and slight, and stood to unhook her bra from behind, finally releasing her breasts and sending a surge of pure X-rated longing through him. He could barely breathe. She was so dainty, her breasts exquisite and small, tipped with rosy peaks. She stepped out of the rest of her clothes gracefully and then stood there, her chest rising and falling because she was breathing so fast.

'You're so beautiful,' Abe said hoarsely. He slipped off the bed, moved to stand in front of her and rested his hands lightly on her shoulders. She looked up at him, her face open and expectant.

'So are you.'

His heart squeezed tight and unbidden words came tumbling out. 'I am really sorry, Georgie, that I was not by your side during your pregnancy and afterwards. You may find my level of duty puzzling but, of course, I would have asked for your hand in marriage then and would have devoted my life to doing whatever it took to secure the well-being of our daughter.'

Georgie noted again how she was rendered a postscript in his drive to do whatever he had to for Tilly's sake, but she wasn't going to reflect on that right now. He'd been right to say that the past, with all its bitterness, had to be put behind them so that their eventual marriage could start in good faith.

Four years ago, he would have asked for her hand in marriage, would have confessed who he really was. Would she have accepted him? Of course, she would have. She would have been hurt that he hadn't told her who he was from the start, but she would have been persuaded by his argument that anonymity had been a prize he hadn't wanted to relinquish because it was as rare as hen's teeth in his world.

'Let's not talk any more.' She skimmed her hands along his waist and then along the rim of his boxers and felt the pulsing of his hardness tenting them.

'You're right, my darling,' he growled. 'We have far more important affairs of state to be getting on with.'

They fell onto the bed, their bodies slickly rubbing together, their hands finding familiar places to caress.

Georgie wriggled her way down, pushing him still with one hand flattened on his chest. She gently licked his nipple with the tip of her tongue and then teased a path with her tongue along his body, tasting the saltiness of his skin and the tightness of muscle and sinew. She ran her fingers lightly along his inner thighs and smiled at his sharp intake of breath.

When she took his bigness in her mouth and darted her tongue along the corded sheath, she wanted to pass out with desire and longing.

Abe had to grit his teeth to stop himself from a headlong rush into release. He looked at the dark cap of her hair as she teased him with her mouth and tongue and then, when he could no longer take the exquisite torture, he manoeuvred her supple body so that he could explore her wetness as she was exploring his hard arousal, so that they could feast on one another.

For Abe, he had the strangest sensation of coming home and he knew that that was because their relationship was on a completely different footing. She was now the mother of his child and as such occupied a special position, one that could be challenged by no one. Naturally that would account for this surge of pleasure and contentment.

He could feel her moving towards a climax. He teased her core with the tip of his tongue and felt its stiffness and the way she moved against his mouth, impatient and desperate for him to go further, to send her hurtling over the edge.

She was by no means alone in this. Never had he felt more aroused.

Oh, but how well he knew her body! Like muscle memory stirring after years of slumber and roaring back into life, he knew just how long to tease her until she was so close to coming that a single thrust was enough to send her over the edge.

He eased her off him and they rearranged themselves with the ease born of familiarity.

Fumbling to locate protection was an obstacle quickly surmounted and when he sank into her, her whole body welcomed him.

Georgie was hanging onto self-control by a thread and that first thrust and then his deeper, second thrust was sufficient to hijack all hope of anything lasting longer than five seconds.

Her orgasm sent her soaring into orbit. Her short nails dug into the small of his back as wave upon wave of pleasure tore through her and she could feel his own orgasm swelling inside her, which turned her on even more.

Her body, dormant for so long, burst into life with the explosive intensity of a dam bursting its banks.

His groan of satisfaction as he came was a blissful sound and when he collapsed onto her, she relished the slickness of his body, damp from exertion.

He rolled onto his side and looked at her with slumberous eyes, then he weaved his fingers through her short hair and smiled.

'I should get dressed,' he murmured. 'My father is very much looking forward to meeting both you and his granddaughter and I have some work to plough through before Tilly and I leave.'

'And I should head to my room, think about having a bath.'

'I don't think so,' he drawled softly. 'This is your suite now. My bed is now our bed, remember? The adjoining door between our suites can be opened so that we both have quick access to Tilly at any time during the day or night.'

Georgie closed her eyes. Their room, their bed…

The sharing of their lives started now because she suspected that their formal union would not be something hastily arranged. As a prince, he would have to have everything in place and that would take time, but in the interim they would be as good as married because she would be sharing his suite, sleeping with him, entering fully into this next phase in her life.

Where would it lead? A shiver of anticipation raced through her and she tried to stifle it because she knew that she would have to bring common sense to bear on this relationship, would have to temper any bursts of optimism that the love she felt might one day be returned with the reality of knowing that they were only here, only together like this, because of Tilly.

But still…

'We'll have to discuss…well, the formal stuff,' she ventured, her voice calm and controlled and interested.

'Royal protocol?' He grinned.

'I suppose so,' Georgie said seriously.

'Life is going to be a great deal less restricted than you imagine,' he told her. 'Tomorrow, I will give you the grand tour. You've seen a section of the palace. There is also a comprehensive gym and two swimming pools, one outdoor and one indoor. The main difference is that anything you want, you will get.'

'That's not necessarily a good thing,' Georgie pointed out, 'and it certainly isn't for a toddler. Tilly will run rings around you if she senses that she can have whatever she wants.'

Abe laughed. He should be heading down to his offices so that he could get some work done before he headed over to his father's palace with Tilly, but when Georgie looked at him the way she was looking at him now, with a mixture of gravity, calm and just a touch of apprehension and self-doubt, he found that all he wanted to do was remain where he was, lying here in bed with her at a crazy time in the middle of the afternoon.

It struck him that whatever advantages he had assumed would be conferred had he married a woman versed in the way of royalty, he could very well have ended up with someone who wouldn't have given a damn about making sure a child of theirs kept their feet firmly adhered to the ground. With vast wealth at their disposal, there would have been the temptation to raise their child to assume automatic superiority and that would have been a serious error of judgement.

'Plus,' Georgie now interjected into the silence, frowning thoughtfully, 'I can't just sit around snapping my fingers and being waited on hand and foot.'

'We have a long conversation ahead of us.' Abe regretfully braced himself to face an hour of work. 'Too long to start now.'

'But we're going to have to have the conversation,' she insisted, squirming into a sitting position against the pillows and watching as he heaved himself off the bed to stare down at her for a few seconds.

The intimacy between them filled her with joy but she realised that being filled with joy because the guy she loved was standing in front of her naked, because he was going to be her husband, wasn't a reason for her to be lulled into following his dictates without question. That would be the start of a very slippery slope.

'Of course we will.' Abe returned her gaze with one equally serious. He moved to perch on the side of the bed. 'You have done an amazing job with Tilly. Do you really think I would stop you from carrying on with that amazing job once we are married? And as for your not sitting around snapping your fingers…' He grinned. 'I can't imagine anyone less likely to be happy doing that.' He stood up, eyebrows raised, but still smiling. 'I can put a time in my diary for us to have this conversation if you like,' he teased. 'Because the expression on your face is telling me that you think it is a conversation I may try to evade.'

'The expression on my face,' Georgie said, 'should be telling you that I am going to be the one giving up everything I've ever known to start a life out here with you, for Tilly's sake. I don't want to think that I'm going to end up floundering because everything I know has been whipped away from under my feet and there are no plans in place for me to have anything at all to call my own or to help me to…adjust to what's going to be a very, very different life.'

'I get that, Georgie.' He raked his fingers through his hair. 'Leave this with me. It will be sorted. There is nothing for you to worry about.'

She nodded but there was a sour taste in her mouth as she remained in the bed as he had a shower, returned to the room, got dressed.

He was so breathtakingly beautiful that she could

feel her reserves of willpower slipping away as she watched him.

How easy it would be to fall completely under his spell all over again, but she would do well to remember that leaving it up to him because he would sort everything and there would be nothing to worry about was much, much easier said than done.

He had nothing to lose. She was in love with him and that was a weakness in itself because it made her susceptible to dreams and hopes that might or might not materialise. The unvarnished truth was that once they were married, she would be vulnerable in a way she wasn't now and, if she had no support network at all, she might end up lost, even if he didn't intend for it to go that way. He would have got everything that he wanted and could she trust him not to sideline her once that happened?

There was a lot inside her that stupidly *did* trust him but, for someone who craved stability, she needed to find a place for herself here, some sort of anchor to hold onto.

Dressed in dark jeans and a white tee shirt, Abe strolled to stand over her. 'You will be fetched when my driver arrives,' he said. 'And you have my cell number. Call if you want anything at all. Shall I get Fatima to bring Tilly in to you? She will need to be introduced to the fact that you and I will now be sharing a bedroom and, no later than tomorrow, we will explain the situation to her, who I am and the way forward.'

Georgie nodded her agreement, dismissing her unsettling thoughts because they weren't going to get her anywhere.

Tomorrow the way forward he had mentioned would begin, but for now she would meet his father and think optimistically about the future even though the comfort zone she had always clung to had been well and truly left behind.

CHAPTER SEVEN

LIFE CHANGED FAST for Georgie. In short order, she met Abe's father, who welcomed her warmly. She thought that again Tilly was a passport to immediate acceptance here, but she refused to dwell on the downsides of that.

If she started dwelling on too many things, then she would quickly reach the conclusion that she was little more than a spare part and she didn't want to question the choices she had made.

The truth was that Tilly was beyond happy. She adored the space, the vast acres of garden, being able to run around, and, more than that, she adored Abe.

They had told her who he was and she had accepted that she now had a dad with the joyful alacrity of a three-year-old too young to really ask any questions.

It was only a matter of days since Georgie had accepted his marriage proposal but the wheels were already turning quickly. Before long, she would meet the team who would be co-ordinating the extravagant wedding. She had also already been introduced to a select number of family members. That number would grow because she would be expected to immerse herself in Abe's world, which was one in which his company seemed to always be in demand.

She had been given a guided tour of the palace by a member of his staff, who had walked several paces behind her as she was shown into every room and the provenance of all the tapestries and mosaic walls and paintings were explained. It had been a slightly unnerving experience.

And, of course, she now had help with Tilly. Plenty of it. More than she actually wanted or needed. She and Tilly still spent time together, but time was no longer something snatched on weekends or after a day working at the hotel. Now, their time together could meander for as little or as long as Georgie liked and then, when she wanted to disappear indoors to cool down by the swimming pool or else read a book or send emails, she could because Fatima or the other nanny would be there to take Tilly off her hands.

There was an eerie sense of limbo about her life and in this limbo, Abe had become her anchor.

He was an attentive partner, a dedicated father and an amazing lover and she knew that being at sea in a different country was playing a part in deepening her love for him.

She thought of him and the feeling of being slightly adrift dissipated.

She couldn't rely on him to sort her life out completely, but he had introduced her to people, and if she still felt lost wandering in his vast palace, then she would get used to it in due course.

The most important thing was her daughter's happiness.

It was apparent that Abe had meant every word he had said when he'd told her that Tilly was the one who mattered in the events that had played out between them.

He would do everything he could to ensure she had a stable and happy life. He was being true to his word thus far and Georgie didn't see why that would change.

But was she more than just part of the package deal?

She hoped so because they continued to get along now that the ammunition had been put away.

And the sex…

She smiled now, thinking about it.

The air sizzled between them. They stepped into the bedroom at night and the heat between them was like a burning inferno. One touch from him and her body responded with scorching urgency.

Right now, at a little after six-thirty in the evening, she was waiting for him in one of the many sitting rooms, this one overlooking the very pool where she had enjoyed a couple of hours earlier with Tilly and Fatima.

She was in a loose-fitting flowered dress with short sleeves that swished to mid-calf. It was one of many new outfits that had been provided for her. A few she had been guided into buying—such as ornate gowns for formal occasions—but she had chosen the rest, along with an assortment of shoes and accessories.

She had drawn the line at jewellery.

'I wouldn't feel comfortable wearing such priceless jewellery on an everyday basis,' she had told Abe two days previously as all manner of rings and necklaces and earrings had been paraded in front of her on beds of purple velvet by the top jeweller in the country. He had been summoned to the palace and had shown his wares with a mixture of deference to the Crown Prince and pride in his vast knowledge of every single gem he had set in front of her for her inspection.

Afterwards, over dinner, Abe had looked at her, his dark eyes amused, and informed her that she was the first woman he had ever met who wasn't interested in jewellery.

'I do love jewellery,' Georgie had responded, blushing when he had rubbed her shin with his bare foot under the table in between the courses that were being ferried out for them from the kitchens, 'but I suppose I'm a little more accustomed to the cosmetic kind when it comes to sticking something on to go to the supermarket.'

'There's no supermarket shopping for you here,' he'd pointed out.

'And I miss that,' she'd said sincerely. 'I never thought I'd miss going to the supermarket, but I do.'

Surprisingly, he had nodded and looked at her thoughtfully. 'I understand.'

'Do you, Abe?' Georgie had asked with genuine

curiosity. 'How can you say that when you've never been to a supermarket in your entire life?'

'Ah, now that's where you're wrong. Don't forget,' he had murmured, skimming his foot along her shin just a tiny bit higher, knowing what her reaction would be, 'that I did go to Cambridge University so I have had some experience of what the inside of a supermarket looks like.'

'Are you sure you didn't have one of your minders running those tedious errands for you?' she had asked wryly, and he had burst out laughing.

'Admittedly it was an irresistible temptation some of the time.'

'I can't believe how spoiled you were.'

'My mother was very down to earth, despite her elevated standing,' Abe had said pensively, in a one-off sharing of confidence, 'I remember that about her, a necessity to instil discipline rather than an easy acceptance of what came with a life of privilege. Unfortunately, when she died, my father retreated into himself for a very long time. He emerged eventually but by then we were both changed irrevocably. I had grown up by myself and he…he substituted the more balanced approach to parenting that my mother had brought to the table with an abundance of material displays of affection. I think it was the only way he could think of handling me. He lacked the spirit to take over where my mother had left off and so, for some years, he replaced this with lavish spending on anything I wanted.'

'That's very sad, Abe. Losing the mother you clearly adored changed everything for both you and your father.' Georgie could empathise; after all, she had also lost her own mother young. She understood why Abe was so keen to protect Tilly and why he felt he would always need to try his hardest to hold back from falling in love himself, as though to repress certain emotions had the power to prevent all hurt. She had been able to see in his expression that it was a time in his young life he was reluctant to dwell on, so she hadn't been at all surprised when he had swiftly brought the topic back to a less emotional angle.

'The minders came as part of the deal,' he had added to lighten the tone. 'Very restricting, hence I did actually take many an opportunity when I was older to venture into supermarkets whenever and wherever I could to purchase something and nothing.'

Georgie had burst out laughing because he could be so funny with an intelligent, dry wit that was pretty irresistible.

'Maybe,' she had mused, 'having lost his wife, he was at pains to make sure he didn't lose you as well, hence the bodyguards to protect you physically and the splurging out materially to try and keep you close. Maybe he thought that, having lost your mother, the last thing you needed might have been too much discipline.'

'You could be right.' His voice had been crisp, winding up the conversation, but he had not been able to hold back from saying, with sadness, 'He could have tried just giving me his time and his companionship and his moral support though...'

He had swiftly moved on from there, back into his own comfort zone of physical contact and Georgie had tactfully not pressed him for any more information.

He was far too proud to have welcomed that approach but when he had opened up to her like that about his past her heart had nevertheless soared and wild hope for more than just 'getting along well' with him had bloomed—even more so when he had also talked to her about his brief time in Ibiza, when he had, for the first time, tasted what *normality* must feel like for most people.

Then he had laughed and shrugged and his eyes had darkened and they had made it to the bedroom mysteriously with their clothes intact because she had never wanted him so badly before.

Were things finally moving in a different direction?

She was smiling at the sound of his feet on the marble flooring and then came that familiar burst of excitement as he appeared in the doorway, knock-out sexy in a pair of linen trousers and a white shirt. The pale colours emphasised the burnished bronze of his skin and the raven darkness of his hair.

He was taking her out to dinner, which would be nice because she was keen to sample some of the different cuisines in the restaurants. As a chef, she was tasting new flavours and combinations every day and she couldn't wait to broaden her scope.

* * *

'You look…amazing,' he said softly, strolling towards her and pausing as she stood up and moved forward.

He reached out and took her hands in his.

She did look amazing. Some kind of loose, floaty dress that managed to conceal everything yet stir the senses in quite an extraordinary way. Her hands were soft in his, her eyes wide and with that guarded look that often underlined her expression.

Would she ever trust him not to hurt her again? he wondered. He had walked out on her once and now she was here and he couldn't help but think that were it not for the fact that he was a prince, she would not have been here at all. Yes, she would have told him about Tilly because she had a strong sense of what was right and what was wrong, but there was a nagging suspicion at the back of his mind that if he had been any old Mr Ordinary, she would have dug her heels in and retained her freedom.

But he wasn't Mr Ordinary and so she had been persuaded into doing what was best for Tilly, even though she had had to walk away from her dreams in the process.

He had been truthful when he had told her that they shared a child who had a right to an upbringing that would only be possible here in Qaram.

Then he had painted an alternative picture of life as it would be should she choose to turn her back on his proposal. He had spared no details and he had watched carefully as she had absorbed what he'd said. So here she was and, while he recognised the importance of making her feel that this was her home, there was no way he could ever give her the fairy-tale life her romantic heart had always craved.

He had witnessed the impact on his father of his mother's death, could remember his own heart-crushing pain at her passing. His duty now lay in running his country, for which great emotional strength was needed and, as far as he was concerned, strength was only possible if you didn't put yourself in the position where you became weak because you'd handed your heart over to someone else for safe-keeping, and it hadn't ended up being kept safe at all. After all, his father had never been the same after his wife had died, and all the pain and misery and stress had ultimately led to a heart attack. So it was up to Abe to make the sacrifices his father had been unable to, in order to be the ruler their country needed.

But within those confines, he would do what it took to make Georgie's life as comfortable as possible and it was a big plus that the chemistry between them continued to burn so strong.

He'd meant what he'd told her—sex and friendship were a better basis for a marriage than anything else.

In life, you couldn't have everything.

'Where are we going?' she asked. 'I hope it's not somewhere too formal, Abe. I'm not sure this dress would do if that's the case...'

'Extremely informal.'

'I didn't realise that princes did informal,' she said, half laughing as they headed out into the main thoroughfare of the palace and following his lead as he asked her about her day and Tilly's.

They left the palace without bodyguards.

Just the two of them piling into a four-wheel-drive Jeep.

'Are you allowed to do this?' she asked as he cruised away from the palace, covering the extensive grounds at a leisurely pace.

It felt intimate here, away from the army of staff, who were practically invisible but not quite invisible enough.

'Do what?'

'Drive alone? Out here?'

He grimaced. 'This is probably one of the safest places on the planet. True, there are occasions when a bodyguard might be a necessity but generally I save the protection for when I'm abroad. I would do without it altogether but Jared, the head of security, worries. Between him and my father, I don't know who panics more easily.'

Georgie relaxed, stared out of the window. It was balmy outside and the windows were down, and the breeze blowing her short hair this way and that made her feel a little drowsy. She slid a surreptitious glance to him. He had one arm loosely hanging over the open window, steering with that hand, and the other casually resting on the gear stick. It was very dark out here now that they had left the palace behind and the green gave way to patchy sandy dunes interspersed with stunted palm trees and in the distance…the sea.

She gazed at the dark landscape, at the distant inky

line of sea. It was a thin black strip against the night sky, which was bejewelled with stars.

Just for a moment Georgie allowed herself the illusion of romance, the illusion that she was with a guy who actually cared about *her* for who she was. They had great sex, shared a child, wined and dined together, but they had never been on a *date* with all the sizzling excitement and breathy hopes for the future that a date implied. This felt like that date.

The Jeep swerved right, heading down towards the black strip of sea, bumping along the dunes, and then banked along a track towards a villa.

'What's this?' She squinted and then, as they got closer, the lights came on outside illuminating a picture-perfect white villa with a red roof, which overlooked the sea.

'It's my bolt-hole.'

'You have a bolt-hole?'

He laughed again, killed the engine and swivelled so that he was looking at her. 'I say *my* bolt-hole. I suppose I should say *our* bolt-hole. I've brought you here because I want you to know that the palace is not the only residence we will occupy. You find it daunting and I can't blame you.'

'I think Tilly rather enjoys it, though.' Georgie smiled. 'She thinks it's a hoot to drive that car of hers along some of the corridors.'

'She does that?' He grinned and slanted a sideways look at her.

'Stop trying to kid me; I've seen you encouraging her, Abe.'

'Why not? It is just a house, after all.' He paused. 'She gets to do what I never did, as it happens. I think this villa will make a refreshing change for you too.'

He was thinking of her. For once she wasn't the postscript following behind his concerns for their daughter, but a concern in her own right, and her heart couldn't help but warm to that idea.

He reached across to open the car door for her.

'Dinner will be here and no one will be in attendance. No one serving the food and pouring the wine. Just the two of us. I had a light meal prepared. It's waiting inside.'

'That's very thoughtful of you, Abe.' Georgie's heart squeezed tight with pleasure and as they walked towards the villa, small by palace standards but still imposing by any normal benchmark, she reached out for his hand and linked her fingers through his.

'You will find that I can be very thoughtful,' Abe murmured.

'I didn't think you were the sort of guy to need a bolt-hole. Why would you need a bolt-hole?'

It was so quiet here, a silent blackness all around them with just the faintest swish of breeze disturbing the endless sea of sand dunes that gave onto the coastline. It was majestic.

'Doesn't everyone?'

'I never saw you as a bolt-hole kind of guy,' she told him, and he laughed as he pushed open the door to let her slide past him.

Georgie stared around her. The villa had been aired and overhead fans swirled a cool breeze against

her skin. The entrance hall was big, but the rich pa-
tina of the wooden floors made it feel warmer and
more inviting than the cold marble in the palace. To
one side, a staircase swept up to a galleried landing
and, ahead, deep, patterned silk rugs led to various
spaces and out, she guessed, to a view of the dunes
rolling down to the sea.

He led her towards the kitchen, where the table
had been set with the finest china and several platters were laid out with lids, which he ceremoniously
opened with exaggerated flourish.

*All this for her... Surely, whether he would admit
it or not, this signalled more than a passing bout of
thoughtfulness?*

'Makes a change, would you not agree?' he asked,
sauntering to the fridge and fetching a bottle of wine
so that he could pour them both a glass.

'A fantastic change.' She sat and watched him and
her heart sped up as he leaned over her, hands clasping the arms of her chair so that she was caged in.

'There is something I would like to say...'

'Is there?' Georgie cleared her throat and longed
for a sip of the wine lying tantalisingly just out of
reach. His fabulous eyes were intent on her face and
sent a wave of colour creeping up her cheeks.

For a few seconds, Abe continued to look at her,
then he moved to one of the chairs and swivelled it
so that he was facing her.

'This is a first for me, Georgie,' he said seriously,
while she hung onto his every word with bated breath
and rising hope.

Would this finally be the declaration of love she had been longing for?

'This villa has always been my own private space because yes, I, like everyone else, enjoy having somewhere to relax, far from the stress of day-to-day life. I have never brought anyone here but I want you to see this as much yours as mine and I would like to suggest that it become our primary residence, with the palace used for more formal occasions. We could have minimum staff and not all the time. You are not in your own home at the moment, and I realise there is a leap to make so I feel that being here might bridge that gap.'

'Ahh…' Georgie pinned a suitably grateful smile on her face and bracingly told herself that he really *had* been thoughtful in bringing her here and offering it as a place where she would certainly feel more comfortable.

But she was alarmed at how fast she had bolted towards a completely different interpretation of what she'd thought he was going to say. There was a lot to be said for taking each day one at a time. Patience was a great virtue and not to be underestimated, as her father used to tell her. *'The hare didn't win the race, the tortoise did.'*

She was a romantic at heart but being a romantic, she decided, was no excuse for being a complete idiot and she wasn't going to let her love for him, and her dependency on him while she found her feet in this strange new world, deter her from having a few guidelines of her own.

'I think it's a fantastic idea, this place for us.' She smiled warmly now. 'You're right. It's a lot less daunting than living in a palace and I've missed…well, having my own space even if that means not having help all the time. I want to get into the kitchen and do some cooking, for a start…'

'Naturally, Fatima will be on call and, indeed, she can live in with us if you'd like. There is a separate suite that would do for housing her.' He paused. 'I have never had any particular longing for the rituals of domesticity but, yes, it would be good to have fewer staff around jumping to our every need. Having a child has certainly opened my eyes to that.'

'There's also something else I should say.'

'Am I going to like it? An opener like that is never followed up by the popping of champagne corks. Talk to me. I'm all ears.'

'You've made a case for us being married, you've persuaded me that it's the right thing to do, that it's the *only* thing to do but…'

'But?'

Georgie hesitated. Was this the right place to have this conversation? The right time? Yet, she knew that she had to tell him what she thought because it was far too easy to let herself fall under his spell and be swept along by a heady combination of sex and her own foolish love.

'This relationship we have… Yes, we get along and, yes, I won't deny that I really enjoy…what we do…together…'

'Sex, Georgie.' He smiled gently. 'We do the raunchiest things in bed and yet you still blush like a virgin when it comes to talking about it. I can't deny how much I enjoy it when you do that.'

'Sex never lasts,' she said flatly.

'It can drop off, in my experience, I agree.'

'And when things change between us…when that eventually fades away, as your wife I will still expect you to remain faithful to me.' She watched him carefully, watched to see any little hesitation, but she could read nothing at all in his expression. His silence propelled her to carry on. 'I don't think I'm asking too much. You may laugh but that was the way I was brought up, to expect fidelity within marriage. I've seen so many cases of what happens when one partner or the other fools around, the damage it causes to their families. You might think that two parents living together, whatever the circumstances of their marriage, is preferable to living apart when it comes to children, but adultery undermines in ways that I would never be able to accept so…'

'You have my word.'

'Oh. Right. Good.' She breathed a sigh of relief.

'There was no need to ask,' he said quietly. 'I have always been a one-woman man.'

'I had to make absolutely sure.'

'You did.' He shrugged. 'And now let us agree that that is something we leave behind. Not only do you have my word on that score, but you also have my word that, should the time ever arrive when I feel myself tempted to stray, then not only will I tell you but I will also give you the option of bailing on our marriage.'

Georgie nodded.

'And the same, naturally, goes for you,' he added mildly. 'What's good for the goose, as you English would say, is good for the gander. What if you are the one who decides to spread your wings?'

'That's not me.'

'How can you be sure, Georgie? I know you were raised with all the right principles in place, but there is nothing in life that is written in stone. When you are surrounded by sand dunes, you quickly understand that what seems hard and fast can change very quickly, depending on the direction of the wind. I've had a lot of experience. You have had precious little. What makes you so sure that you won't start wondering what other excitement lies out there, as yet untested?'

'You truly don't know me if you think that,' she said with conviction.

'In that case, like I said, let's leave it there and enjoy the feast that's been prepared. Afterwards, I will give you a guided tour. You'll be excited to know that it'll take a fraction of the time it took for you to become acquainted with the palace.'

Georgie relaxed. He might not love her—*yet*—the way she loved him, but he was committed to what they were doing. He wouldn't decide that boredom might be a good excuse to stray and she believed what he had told her.

They both had principles.

The food was exquisite. They camped at the kitchen table and she enjoyed every mouthful. Sitting opposite him, she couldn't help but stare at his outrageous beauty and be lulled by his anecdotes as he described his country to her and its history. The sex might fade at some far distant point in the future, but right now she was turned on just at the anticipation of being in bed with him later tonight.

He showed her round the villa. The paintings were bold and colourful, and he explained that they were all done by local artists. He reminded her of her love of painting, of the sketchbook she used to carry around with her all those years ago in Ibiza. He remembered the cloth case she had used for her charcoals.

There was an arts council, he told her, and she could get involved with it. He explained who worked on it and how she could contribute to growing it.

She'd asked him how on earth she was going to orient herself when she knew no one and he was answering that question now and just the thought of finding some kind of footing was incredibly calming.

In the relaxed, informal atmosphere at the villa, without staff, they discussed the minutiae of their arrangements.

Social engagements, the whens and whys and wherefores, Tilly's schooling, Georgie's apartment in London—which she would have liked to have kept but which he vetoed very firmly and, though she wanted to dig her heels in for some vague reason, she honestly couldn't come up with a good enough reason to argue the toss.

* * *

In the quiet of his villa, Abe tried to work out what she was thinking. He had predicted that she would like the villa, the peace, the proximity to the sea and, by daylight, the stunning views of ocean and sand.

He had used the opportunity to discuss all those things that somehow hadn't been raised in any depth thus far and she had listened and accepted what he said with surprisingly little objection.

He hadn't liked that, but he had no idea what to do about it and, from every angle, he was assailed by guilt at what she was giving up for him, even though he knew that he had nothing to feel guilty about.

He wasn't going to promise anything he couldn't deliver and all he could and *would* deliver would be a lifestyle she might enjoy in time.

'No need to tidy up,' he said, more harshly than intended, as she made to clear the dishes once they'd finished. 'It will be done when we leave.'

She blushed and shrugged and he stared at her, frowning and not quite knowing how to ease the tension that had sprung up out of nowhere.

There was one obvious way to regain their equilibrium. *His* comfort zone.

He slipped his arm around her waist and pulled her to him, and as she was teetering and beginning to laugh he swept her off her feet and began walking to the door while she clung to him, and he felt the tension ease right out of her, as he'd hoped it would.

'Time to get back to the palace.' He nuzzled her

neck and she squealed and then rubbed her cheek against his six o'clock shadow. 'I have needs and talking isn't one of them…'

CHAPTER EIGHT

'TOMORROW, THE NEWSPAPERS will be running the happy news of our impending marriage.' This the following morning as they were having breakfast on the patio with Tilly between them, squirming on her chair and reeling off a non-stop battery of questions, mostly pertaining to the swimming pool and when she could get to it.

'I thought everyone already knew about us… Tilly…' No sooner had she come to terms with one staging post, Georgie thought, than she found herself confronted by another.

She had travelled to Qaram to acquaint both herself and Tilly with the country she'd thought their daughter would be visiting a couple of times a year.

Had she expected to end up sleeping with Abe? No. Had she spent years living with the bitterness of knowing that he had used her and dumped her without a backward glance? Yes!

But it felt as if the ground had shifted under her feet without her even really realising.

Abe had re-entered her life and had managed to

disentangle her fingers from every single thing she had been clinging to ever since she had met him.

He had blown a hole in the little life she had built for herself and now she was due to be his wife, meeting people she would never have met before, living a life she had never dreamt conceivable.

Bitterness had been no protection for her heart. Bit by bit, she had fallen for him all over again and this time there was no sense that it might be infatuation. They shared a child and what she felt now was deep and strong. But how many more deep breaths would she have to take to face up to yet another challenge she hadn't banked on?

The thought of the town crier publicising their impending marriage made her feel like a character from a Disney movie, but this was rarefied life as few knew it.

'Protocol,' he returned succinctly. 'Tilly, are you going to eat that bread or are you going to play with it?'

'Play with it?' Tilly responded hopefully. 'I want to have a swim. I'm hot!'

Georgie looked at her daughter, so different from when they had been living in London. Now, Tilly was livelier, more energetic, more curious. Under the blazing sun, her skin had turned a burnished bronze, just like her dad's, and she looked the picture of health.

Nursery every day and snatched playtimes before bed and on the weekends…those things were gone. More than that, though, was the joy of Tilly having a father who, true to his word, geared his day towards making sure he spent some quality time with his daughter.

And wasn't that good for *her* as well? Georgie thought. Having someone there to share the responsibilities? Not just that, but having someone who found as much pleasure in the small, funny things Tilly said and did?

She loved everything about this man and yet there was still a pool of uncertainty somewhere deep inside that she had signed her life over to a guy who had not once said anything to her that might have given her any idea that she was loved.

'Lessons first, Tilly, and then pool after.' Lessons involved a lovely young girl who came in to teach and already Tilly, who was bright as a sparrow, was beginning to learn the basics of reading and the foundations of the language that would become her own in due course.

When the new term began, she would attend school, a battle easily won by Georgie because, although Abe had been home-tutored, he was far more in favour of the routine of school and the benefits of friendship with peers that it brought.

She absently watched as Tilly skipped off with Fatima, having given her a hug, but she was frowning when she looked at Abe. He tossed his linen serviette on the table, shoved his chair at an angle so that he could extend his legs to one side and looked right back at her with raised eyebrows.

'Something on your mind, Georgie?'

'No.' She looked away, out to the pleasing panorama of tended green with its distant horizon of tan sands.

'Spit it out.'

'You should get off to work.' She tried a smile on for size but he refused to buy into it.

'Work can wait.'

'So there will be no turning back once it hits the headlines,' she mused, gazing past him. 'Feels odd, I suppose. Just when I get accustomed to the thought of me and you…of *us*… I now have to gear myself up for a press conference about it.'

'Was there going to be any turning back for you?' Abe wondered if a time would come when her doubts would be banished for ever. After she was wearing his ring? How many more times would he have to persuade her into truly believing him when he told her that they had the makings of a very successful union?

He looked at her, so slender, chewing her lip anxiously, a vision of feminine prettiness in a short-sleeved pale yellow tee shirt and a light skirt. She brought out an intensely protective urge in him. She was the mother of his child so that was perfectly understandable. Frustrated, he raked his fingers through his hair and continued to gaze at her.

'No, but—'

'Then where is the problem?'

'There are still so many things to put into place.'

'You worry too much.'

'Of course I do! Can you blame me? It's a big

step and now it feels…' She sighed helplessly and he reached out and threaded his fingers through hers.

'The hotel knows.' Abe decided that ticking her various concerns off the checklist might be the best way forward. It made him smile, which was odd because he had never had much time for moody female behaviour. In Georgie, it excited and challenged him; it was that simple. She would never bore him.

'Yes. I spoke to my friend there and we had a long chat about everything. It was good of you to break the news.'

'You were dithering. Your flat…that's in the process of being sold. You said you wanted the money you got from it to be transferred to your next-door neighbour who helped you over the years with Tilly? It'll be done.'

'That's a great help. I'm not sure how I would have managed it from over here.'

'We have discussed the details about Tilly's schooling. The arts council? They are ready and overjoyed to have your input when you feel you would like to go along…' He paused. 'This meet-and-greet with the press is simply a formality, Georgie. Nothing to get unduly exercised about.'

'I suppose it's the feeling that everything is rushing towards me and I can't put up any stop signs, not that I *want* to…'

'But you feel safe as long as you think your options are being kept open,' Abe finished astutely, and she nodded. 'And seeing it in print makes you anxious.'

She nodded again.

'Like I said, it'll be a formality. The toughest part you have already dealt with and that was meeting my father, members of my family, my friends. And bear in mind that it will not be marriage overnight. I will be expected to have a lavish wedding with a guest list of hundreds, hence the fact that we won't actually tie the knot for another month or so. Trust me, by the time we exchange vows, all your anxieties will have been vanquished.'

'How can you be so sure of everything?' she asked, but she had relaxed and was half smiling.

'No one can be sure of everything,' Abe murmured, 'but it's fair to say that I usually am and I'm usually right.' He stood up, held his hand out for her. The coolness of her fingers entwined with his sent a jolt of red-hot lust through him, but he gritted his teeth and fought off that now familiar craving to take her, however inconvenient the timing might have been.

'Thank you for that reassurance, Abe,' Georgie said drily. 'It's good to know that I'm with someone who is always right.'

'Isn't it?' He dealt her a slashing sidelong grin that sent shivers through her. 'Now I have to get to work so don't tempt me.'

'Tempt you to do what?' Georgie smiled innocently.

'I'll show you tonight…'

The following morning, Georgie woke to an empty room. They had made passionate love the night before and she had obviously fallen into a deep sleep because she hadn't heard Abe leaving the bedroom and neither had she been awakened by Tilly toddling in demanding cuddles.

She glanced at her phone, realised that it was nearly nine in the morning and, with a yelp of dismay, she leapt out of bed, flung on her dressing gown and burst into the adjoining suite to find Abe and Tilly in the process of choosing clothes for Tilly to wear.

'I overslept!' She tugged her dressing-gown belt tightly round her waist and gazed at the array of outfits scattered across the floor. 'What's all this about?'

'Is it not a lady's prerogative to choose what she wants to wear?' Abe, sitting on the ground with his long legs stretched out in front of him, looked at his daughter with tender indulgence. 'She's been fed and watered, and Fatima is going to collect her in half an hour to take her to my father's palace. She's going to meet some of the children who will also be attending her school next term. We will join everyone after the reporters are through with us.'

'Oh, good heavens, I'd completely forgotten about that.'

'No need to panic. It is not for another couple of hours. Join us. We were debating which outfit might be most appropriate for meeting other toddlers. Right now, the pink ballet dancer one appears to be in the lead.' He pointed to a confection of pink lace and silk that had mysteriously appeared in Tilly's wardrobe a few days ago.

As she looked at them both there on the ground the

scene could not have been more natural, more heart-warming, and only his reminder that a bunch of re-porters would be congregating in a couple of hours to take photos of them signalled just how unusual her new reality really was.

Photos of them both smiling for the camera would be published in one form or another across the world. Not only would everyone at the hotel where she had worked see them, but eventually, when they appeared in the weekly glossy magazines her friends back home read, they too would be agog to see her on the arm of a drop-dead gorgeous prince.

Oblivious to her mother's panic, Tilly was reach-ing to hold up the ballet tutu and Georgie marvelled that this was a world her daughter would become so accustomed to that in time the flashbulbs of cameras pointing at her would be accepted as part and parcel of the life she led.

For the first time, Georgie really appreciated what Abe had meant when he had urged her to marry him because it was important that Tilly claim a legacy that was her right by birth and was protected while she did so.

It seemed crazy that she had ever imagined that things could be normal had Tilly moved from one country to another, from a flat in London to a pal-ace in Qaram. She would have been utterly confused.

'Tilly.' Georgie stepped forward and smiled at her daughter, who looked at her quizzically. 'Why not go for the flowered dress and the sandals?'

'Boring,' was the immediate response.

'Argumentative like her mother,' Georgie said as Abe grinned and looked at her with lazy amusement.

For a while, Georgie forgot the stress ahead of her and got into the spirit of choosing something for Tilly to wear, and Tilly, in the thick of all the attention, was in her element.

They were laughing when, twenty minutes later, Fatima arrived to gather up a delighted Tilly, who had compromised with half the ballet outfit, sporting a tutu and ballet pumps with a flowered cotton tee shirt.

'Will you be working until…the photo shoot?' There was still the ghost of a smile on Georgie's face as she closed the door behind Fatima and Tilly and turned to look at Abe, who was rising to his feet and stepping over the scattered discarded outfits to move towards her.

In faded jeans and a tee shirt, he was utterly casual and utterly gorgeous.

She stared and sucked in her breath when he was standing right in front of her.

Would she ever, she wondered, be able to be close to this man without her entire nervous system going into freefall? Was this all part of the package deal when you fell in love with someone? She'd thought all the disillusionment she had suffered at his hands four years previously might have stood her in good stead when it came to securing her defences against him. She'd been wrong.

'I will,' Abe said gravely. 'But just for the moment…' he lightly held the edge of her silky dressing gown between two fingers and smiled '…the glimpse of an errant breast has managed to catch my attention.'

'What are you talking about?'

Georgie stared down to see that, between her lifting Tilly up and closing the door when Fatima had come to sweep her away, the dressing-gown belt had loosened so that she was a little less decent than she'd thought she was.

He slipped his fingers underneath the thin silk and stroked the soft swell of her breasts and then gently, absently brushed a finger over her nipple, which stiffened in immediate response.

He kissed her. A long, slow and tender kiss that made her melt and, with a soft little moan, she reached up on tiptoe to return the kiss, loving the wet melding of their tongues.

His kiss deepened and she didn't have to feel the rigid bulge to know that he was turned on—she could hear it in his roughened groan. He pulled apart the dressing gown, underneath which she was just in a pair of knickers, and it slithered to the ground in a pool of pale green and blue.

Georgie arched up into his embrace and he cupped her buttocks, driving her against him, urging her to swing up to wrap her legs around his waist.

It was an invisible communication, a barely felt touch, and Georgie automatically did just that and hugged him close as he carried her into the bedroom and laid her down on the bed, but when she would have squirmed up against the pillows, he stayed her and positioned her so that she was lying on the bed with both legs hanging off.

Heady with anticipation, Georgie looked down as he knelt in front of her. He eased the knickers off and discarded them, attention remaining firmly focused on the delicate triangle of hair between her thighs.

The gentle slide of his tongue, finding the groove that sheathed her womanhood, evinced a low moan of pure pleasure from her.

He kept her thighs spread with the flattened palms of his hands and tasted her the way someone might taste the most delicate and fragrant of morsels. He licked and delved and licked again until Georgie was going crazy with wanting more, but he wouldn't let her squirm away from his questing tongue.

Instead, he continued to lick, to tease the tight bud with the tip of his darting tongue, and when he inserted his finger deep into her, she couldn't stop herself. The slow build to an orgasm accelerated with the speed of a supersonic rocket and she came against his mouth in long, shuddering spasms of intense, exquisite pleasure.

She looked down at his dark head between her legs and reached to curl her fingers in his lush hair.

'Abe…'

'You're way too good at distracting me,' he growled.

Their lovemaking was fast and intense. Georgie clung to Abe; the feel of him filling her, the rub of his hardness against the still tender, engorged parts of her, sent waves of deep satisfaction coursing through her.

She could have stayed there with him for ever, could have held him close and lain with him while time passed by, but with less than a couple of hours to get ready she flew into preparation mode like a bat out of hell.

'I'll leave you to it,' he said. 'I have some work to get through and I will change in my offices and meet you back here in an hour. There isn't a huge amount of time, I know, but...'

'But that's what happens when you lose focus.'

'I could not have said it better myself.'

That said, Georgie thought, flying through a shower and then flinging open her wardrobe doors to inspect which of the, as yet, unworn formal dresses she would put on, hot, hard sex had certainly had the desired effect of squashing all of her nerves. She just didn't have the time to feel anything but rushed!

She opted for something that could weather the blazing heat that would confront her once she was standing outside the palace where, Abe had informed her, the photo shoot would take place.

She was becoming accustomed to the temperatures, which soared during the day and only really became comfortable once the sun had dipped away.

Dressing for the sun here bore no resemblance to dressing for the sun in London.

Thirty-five minutes later, she looked at her reflection in the floor-to-ceiling mirror in the bedroom.

The dress was modest, with loose sleeves in shades

of apricot. It was pleasingly Grecian in style and designed to repel the intense heat. Strangely, it often paid to wear loose clothes that covered you up practically from head to toe when it came to combating the temperatures the minute you stepped foot outdoors.

He had said he would fetch her and when he did, it occurred to Georgie that she'd had no idea what he would be wearing. A pair of light trousers? Linen? A shirt? One of those handmade white ones with the royal insignia embroidered in tiny letters? He had wardrobes full of them. She hadn't expected him in traditional white robes, but he was, and the sight of him took her breath away. She was vaguely aware of him saying something complimentary to her but she didn't really take it in. She was too busy staring, and in the end, embarrassed, she cleared her throat and made an attempt to focus.

'Ready?'

'As ready as I'll ever be.' She walked towards him, still blushing.

He looked what he was: a prince, a man who could change lives, who held the reins of supreme power in his hands. He held out his arm for her and she took it. Her heart was pounding as she headed out of the room and then down the sweeping staircase at the bottom of which various members of staff had gathered.

All that was missing was a red carpet. The front doors were pulled open and a waft of hot air engulfed her and she blinked at the bank of photographers waiting for them to emerge.

Her fingers tightened on his forearm and he patted her gently, completely in control of the situation.

There was no pushing or shoving. Everything was orderly and she knew that she was smiling although her nervous system had kicked into fifth gear, more than making up for the previous lull.

'Relax,' he murmured, sotto voce, and she forced herself to try and unbend a bit.

Faces behind long lenses were arranged in banks—far more than she had expected. Surely there were photographers and reporters who weren't just from Qaram? It was astonishing that she had not realised, from the very first moment she'd discovered Abe's true identity, just what a huge deal this whole situation was going to be.

Her body was as rigid as a plank of wood. His exhortation to her to relax could not have fallen on deafer ears.

She was barely aware of his arm sliding around her waist or of him turning to look down on her but then, suddenly, there were just the two of them. Everything else, the heat, the cameras, the people—all of it disappeared and became background noise because all she could see were his dark, dark eyes and the sensuous curve of his mouth. All she could feel was the warm reassurance radiating out from him towards her.

He smiled long and low and she practically melted as he bent to capture her mouth, gently inserting his tongue, tasting her and demanding a response in return, which she was all too happy to give.

She curled her hands around his neck and linked her fingers together, her body moulding gently against his. When he pulled back, she blinked, momentarily disoriented.

'Now, *that's* more like it,' he said, smiling. '*Now* you're relaxed.'

Yes, now she really was relaxed and so completely in love that she couldn't tear her eyes away from his face. She'd been nervous as a kitten and he had put his arms around her and made her feel safe. That was how he made her feel time and again. Safe. It shouldn't make sense, not when she'd spent years hating him, not when she knew that this marriage on the cards was little more than a business arrangement, and yet he still made her feel safe, as though what was happening between them couldn't have been more right.

Looking down at her upturned face, Abe, for one fleeting second, was sucked into the crazy illusion that this was the real thing. Her eyes were shining. She looked like…like the queen she would very soon become, and it was nothing to do with the clothes she wore or her physical attractiveness.

There was a kindness and a generosity there that gave her a regal aura of which she was touchingly unaware. It was a modesty that hailed from her background, Abe thought. As the daughter of a vicar, an only child and one who had lost her own mother at a young age, she had been raised to put others before herself. It was why she had told him about Tilly, why she could never be bought with money or status, why she had been persuaded into marrying him.

He had been struck dumb when she had opened that bedroom door to him. He was so used to seeing her casually dressed, to see her dressed for the part had stopped him dead in his tracks. Had she noticed? She had looked perfect for the role as his wife-to-be.

Even now, standing here, with the sun pouring down on them and the sound of cameras clicking, Abe could *feel* the warmth and benevolence of the journalists and photographers in front of them.

This was a woman who deserved the best that life had to offer and he was not equipped to give that to her.

He might be able to give her fame and fortune, and he could shower her in jewels and grant her every material wish, but what about those other wishes? The ones she deserved? He couldn't grant those. He was a man who had locked his heart away and thrown away the key and it was only fair that he did not allow her to harbour any illusions on that score.

He'd hurt her once, four years ago and he wasn't going to hurt her again. This was a truth written on stone, as far as he was concerned.

However, uneasy with this train of thought, Abe focused on the here and now and on the crowd in front of them.

He would think things through, navigate a way forward that would be fair on Georgie. That look in her eyes as she had gazed up at him, that soft smile playing on her mouth, those things had told a story and he did not want that story to end in a place where she believed that promises were being made that he knew would never be delivered.

Their fingers were entwined and he squeezed her hand supportively before withdrawing his and was proud and pleased that she did what was expected. No woman bred for this very purpose, no woman with all the right credentials, could have done better.

After half an hour, he bowed and announced, in a good-natured voice, that that was it for the day.

Questions were posed and he answered a couple of them but was already turning away, hand moving to the small of her back, urging her back into the cool of the palace.

'Was it as bad as you thought?' was the first thing he asked when they were inside. 'I should tell you that you acquitted yourself with aplomb.'

'Thank you.' Georgie reddened with pleasure. 'I'd expected more of a scrum, to be honest.' He was heading in the direction of one of the sitting areas, a room that was less chillingly formal than most of them, tucked away to the side and overlooking the gardens at the back. 'What is the plan now? When will we leave to go and see your father?'

Fresh juice had been laid out ahead of their arrival and Abe poured them both a glass. It had been a good morning and a good photo shoot, and it would be criminal to spoil things now by launching into another heart-to-heart on marital expectations. Did he really have to spell things out for her again in black and white? Wasn't that a bit crass? He'd been very open on the day she'd agreed to marry him, that love played no part in their future, and still she'd agreed to marry him. Could he have been mistaken about that look in her eyes when she had gazed up at him?

Actions, he decided, always spoke louder than words. If she were to be travelling in the direction of expecting love and all the complications associated with it, then wouldn't it be more hurtful to give a long speech on what she shouldn't expect? She was astute. Wouldn't it be better to *show* her what he meant by how he behaved instead? Wouldn't that approach be more subtle? Less humiliating for her? Kinder?

When Abe thought about hurting her, the ache he felt deep, deep inside was almost physical, which only reinforced his decision that this was the right way forward.

'I'll change first.' He grimaced. 'These clothes feel restrictive even though they're loose.'

'Okay.' Georgie smiled. He had offered her some juice, which was very refreshing, and then he had stepped back, away from her.

Was it her imagination or was there a certain polite remoteness to him now that the business of the photo shoot was over and done with?

He had kissed her, and she had lost herself in that kiss, but it hadn't escaped her notice that he had let go of her hand immediately afterwards.

No matter. She was way too sensitive about…everything.

The bottom line was that the photo shoot had been

fun. There had been no attacking questions and everyone had seemed delighted that their Prince was due to marry, that he was a father, that a love that had been lost had been miraculously restored. Serendipity. It was an assumption Abe had not denied.

'And now that the cat's out of the bag…life is going to get even more hectic, I am afraid.'

'What do you mean?'

'Parties, events, social engagements…there is one the day after tomorrow. Nothing too fancy but it will be a good opportunity for you to meet some of the people we will be socialising with.'

Parties…events…social engagements…

The pace was stepping up, Georgie thought, but she smiled and relaxed. Why would she be scared? Wasn't Abe going to be by her side?

CHAPTER NINE

TILLY WAS WHIRLING round and round the room, half dressed, pretending to be a pirate from one of the books Abe repeatedly read to her on a nightly basis. It had captured her imagination but unfortunately was a high energy game and right now Georgie needed to get her daughter dressed and ready to leave for the party Abe had told her about only a couple of days previously.

Since then she had seen little of him because he had been out of the country, but they had spoken and it seemed that the informal do was something of an official engagement party, which his father would be hosting.

It was clear that their idea of 'informal' differed greatly, because he had informed her, as a postscript, that there would be in the region of sixty people attending.

'It was hurriedly arranged,' he had explained the night before when he had called her, 'but my father was excited after the photo shoot and there was curiosity all round, if I am honest. I did try to talk him into a less rushed time schedule, but he was having none of it.'

So now here she was trying to capture the bundle of energy that was her daughter because both of them would have to get ready. They would be driven to his father's palace where she would meet Abe, who would come straight from the airport.

The thought of seeing Abe again after only a couple of days without him filled Georgie with excitement. It felt as though he had been away for months, *years*. She had chosen what she was going to wear carefully and, yes, she knew what was expected of her on the sartorial front, but she also knew what he liked and she had gone for a deep burgundy dress that framed her slender body like a glove while remaining perfectly decent, because the figure-hugging, contoured sheath was superimposed under layers of transparent, pale pink voile and silk that floated around her in an extremely flattering manner.

Two weeks ago, she would have been a bag of nerves but that was then. Now, things had subtly changed.

She grabbed Tilly, subjected her to a series of kisses and tickles and frogmarched her to the bathroom, where she bribed her into the bath with a selection of toys and her favourite bubble bath.

She chatted and sang and played but her mind absently darted across the landscape that had become her life, against all odds.

The confusion and panic she had felt when she had first arrived in Qaram had ebbed away and in its place was a contentment she had never expected to feel. She wasn't an outsider, but someone who had been welcomed into a country that was not her own. She had had to rely on Abe and he had been true to his word. He had guided her every step of the way, slowly integrating her into his way of life.

She had been dogged for so long by fear of change. Life had changed for her when her mother had died but, over time, that void had been filled by her dad, the crack in her life papered over, but then he had died, leaving her on her own, and although she had jumped ship to go to Ibiza, in an attempt to lose herself in something new and different and challenging, she had never stopped craving stability.

Having Tilly had propelled Georgie into a life where no chances were taken because someone else had been depending on her, relying on her not to guide her into unsteady waters.

So Abe, coming back into her life like an invading storm, had filled her with trepidation.

Every step she had taken had been difficult as she had been edged away from her bone-deep desire for security into a world where she no longer knew the rules.

She need not have worried because Abe had been there for her. Was it any wonder that she couldn't think of him without smiling? They were perfect together. They were perfect in bed and they were perfect out of it as well.

So there were no loud declarations of love. That just wasn't his style. She had seen enough to hope that he cared for her as deeply as she cared for him, whether he realised it or not. She was also hoping that the two days spent apart might have awakened some recognition in him of what he felt for her.

Had he missed her? He certainly seemed to show a keen interest in how she was spending her time in his absence. He had told her to do whatever she wanted to the villa, to make whatever changes she wanted, so that it would feel like home.

At the moment, they were still living in the palace, but as soon as they were married they would decamp to the villa, and he was keen that she had a hand in kitting it out. She had felt a flair of excitement at the thought of that. She had already started planning on redoing and expanding the kitchen, and maybe even putting in a studio, because the light pouring in from the ocean was fantastic for painting. Who knew? Perhaps she could resurrect her vanished career as an illustrator for kids' books... At any rate, she could illustrate for a book for Tilly, which would be nice.

Tilly would miss the vast playroom with the miniature village, but there would be a pool and walks on the beach at sunset. Like Cornwall. At a stretch.

She managed to dress Tilly in an outfit not of her choosing, the fairy confection sidelined in favour of a far more subdued dress and sandals. Fatima whipped her away to give her some dinner then, leaving Georgie an hour and a half to get dressed, which she did slowly and carefully.

A long, luxurious bath and then make-up and then the outfit. It was a little after six and the driver would be delivering them to Basha's palace for six forty-five. Abe would be there and she was fired up to see him, already looking forward to a night of heady passion after the party.

She slipped her feet into delicate, strappy sandals that elevated her height to a very respectable five eight and she and a very excited Tilly were ready and waiting for Abe's driver, Sid, to arrive for them.

She felt good. She felt excited. She felt like a woman in love, and the little voice in her head that had kept repeating that that was a very foolish way to feel had become fainter and fainter over time.

There would be children of Tilly's age there to play with. A few she had already met. Like most young kids, and perhaps because she had become accustomed to the sociability of being in a nursery from a very young age, Tilly had no qualms when it came to making friends.

They arrived at the palace and Tilly could barely contain her excitement at seeing two of the kids she had met only recently. Georgie knew what the routine was likely to be. All the young children would be proudly paraded in front of people for a short while and then whooshed off to one of the rooms in the palace where they would be supervised until, one by one, they eventually fell asleep.

The palace was decorated lavishly, especially considering the very short notice.

But then, an army of people could go a long way when it came to making sure the details were all picture-perfect even though time was limited.

There were small lights blazing on all the trees that led to the courtyard in front of the palace. The palace itself shone as bright as a Christmas tree and the front doors had been thrown open and were guarded by a uniformed man on either side. High-end cars were parked neatly to one side, disappearing into the darkness at the back, and people were entering, formally dressed, many of the men in traditional outfits.

Georgie felt a pang of intense nerves but excitement at the thought of seeing Abe overcame whatever anxiety she was feeling.

The door was opened for her and Tilly flew out but then stopped dead in her tracks at the sight of everyone and turned to Georgie to be lifted up.

So that was how Georgie entered the palace, as people fell back to let her through and one of the members of staff hurried forward to guide a path straight to Abe—with Tilly wrapped up in her arms, wreaking havoc with the dress and ruining the classy entrance she had hoped for, where Abe would turn to look at her and wouldn't be able to look away.

There was no music but there was a lot of laughter and talking and buzz. Dozens of waiters were working the crowded room, serving drinks and nibbles on huge circular platters.

Georgie was stopped so many times along the way that she lost count. She'd personally met very few of the guests but Qaram was small and, now that she and Abe were officially pronounced a couple in the eyes of the world, everyone was keen to get to know her.

She smiled and nodded and chatted and felt more

at ease than she'd expected. English might not have been the first language for many there, but they were all fluent in it and they all seemed to share the same keenness to put her at her ease.

Having finally deposited Tilly on the ground and straightened her dress, she looked up and there he was, standing towards the back of the room with a drink in his hand, surrounded by a little cluster of men, who all looked like businessmen.

He was staring directly at her, and Georgie felt her heart do a little tap dance inside her, then she smiled and began weaving her way towards him.

He simultaneously moved towards her as well, excusing himself from the group of men to whom he had been chatting about a Pharma deal and what it could do for the country.

She looked stunning, he thought. Of course she did. When she'd walked in with Tilly in her arms, she'd embodied, for him, the essence of motherhood and his chest had positively swollen with pride.

Her smile, when she'd spotted him, had been spontaneous and wide and filled with delight and, remembering his resolution, he had stood firm against the temptation to smile back at her.

He had had a couple of days away from her to really think things over and the more he thought, the more he came to the conclusion that it was important not to encourage her into thinking that there could ever be more to what they had than what was there already. Good sex, friendship, and shared adoration of their daughter.

She'd told him that sex faded in time. He wasn't so sure it would in their case. It was certainly going as strong as it ever had been and if it ever faded? They would still maintain their shared warmth and camaraderie. It would be enough.

In the meanwhile, it would be important to make sure they were both on the same page.

'I tried your mobile,' he said, drawing her to one side, 'to let you know that I had arrived, but there was no answer.'

'I forgot it at home,' Georgie confessed. 'It was all very calm to start with but then suddenly it was a mad dash and I didn't think to bring it.' She was disappointed that he had not commented on her dress, on how she looked, but then it was a busy evening for him and he would be tired, no doubt, having just flown in from abroad.

'You know the routine for tonight?'

'Sorry?'

'The procedure?'

'Well…yes…' Georgie glanced around. Everyone seemed to be having a good time, which, she thought, was the main thing.

'I sent you an email this morning. Did you get around to reading it?'

'No. Tell me what it said. Have I dressed inappropriately?' She glanced around again but, no, surely she wasn't overdressed or underdressed?

'You look fine. It is about the seating arrangements for the dinner. You will be responsible for ushering everyone through to the dining hall. A member of staff will alert you to when seating arrangements have to commence. My father will sit at one end of the table and I will be at the other end. You will be next to me bar one.'

Fine? Was that all he had to say on the subject of the outfit she had been at great pains to choose in the expectation that it would please him?

And now here he was, outlining how the next few hours should unfold, reminding her in no uncertain terms that this might be a party to celebrate their forthcoming union, but it was also an event she would have to oversee in her role as his wife-to-be.

Georgie felt her previous heady excitement cool.

'Of course,' she said a little stiffly.

'I am going to see Tilly now.' He smiled and Georgie thought that it was the first time he had really smiled since laying eyes on her this evening.

'I managed to talk her down from the fairy outfit. She's very sensibly dressed for the occasion, although she did insist on travelling with a bag of toys…'

Abe burst out laughing. 'I wonder if those toddlers in there have the faintest idea who is going to be running rings around them in the years to come,' he mused. He glanced at his watch, looked at her and she took the hint immediately.

Time to do her duty, to mingle and socialise and wait for the appointed time when she would have to usher everyone towards the dining area for the extensive sit-down meal.

There should have been some hitches. Weren't there always at an event like this, especially one that had been hurriedly cobbled together at the very last minute thanks to Basha's insistence?

Thankfully, there were none.

People chatted and voices grew louder and the nibbles that were passed round were amazing. Georgie thought about the snacks she had trolleyed up to that hotel room on the day she had seen Abe again for the first time. It seemed like a lifetime ago now.

She checked in on Tilly three times, the last time to find her sound asleep on one of the brightly coloured modular sofas that were low enough to be completely child friendly.

She managed to grab a few sentences with Basha over the course of the evening, congratulating him on organising the event in such a short space of time, and was thrilled when he responded by telling her that it meant the world to him that everyone, friends and family alike, could get to meet the girl who would become his daughter-in-law.

The food was amazing and, sandwiched between the chair of the arts council and a distant relative of Abe's, she felt that it was a successful evening.

But how much had she seen of Abe?

Virtually nothing at all. He had briefly chatted to her when she'd arrived and then he had promptly left her to her own devices for the remainder of the evening and when, eventually, she *had* seen him because he had been sitting close to her at the dinner table, he had shot her a reassuring smile, raised his eyebrows in a silent question, asking her if all was going well, and then, again, had promptly turned his attention to the attractive brunette next to him.

For the first time since she had arrived in Qaram, Georgie felt that she was getting a glimpse of what life would look like in the weeks and months and years to come. The hand-holding had come to a close and this was now her end of the bargain, to fulfil her duties as his wife, without the emotional reserves there to bolster her because underneath the 'rubbing along nicely' was a void that would never be filled. He would have her back, because she was Tilly's mother and because that was his obligation, but if she'd thought that he would be the one to offer her love and support, someone who would feel her doubts and sometimes her insecurities and ache for her because she meant the world to him, then she'd been kidding herself.

Her job would be to acquit herself well and he would be proud of her. They would have sex and, for him, everything would be just as he wanted it to be. Would he stray? He had a high libido and there was no doubt that, married or not, he would have a million women ready and willing to sleep with him, but he would expect them to continue being lovers and so why would he stray if by doing so he risked Georgie leaving him, thereby jeopardising his daughter's security?

She would have wished her dreams away on a man

who was incapable of giving her the love she wanted, and for the first time she felt that fact truly hit home for her. Dreams and hopes and reading into things had turned the need for pragmatism into lovesick compliance, against all of her best instincts.

A trickle of unease filtered through her, but she kept going until the last guest had gone, at which point Abe went to fetch Tilly from where she was still sound asleep, and still sleeping in exactly the same position as she had been three hours previously. She literally hadn't moved so much as a finger.

It was a little after midnight.

Many of the relatives were staying at the palace with Basha. Others had been ferried away in chauffeur-driven cars, which had begun circling the courtyard just before midnight, waiting for their clients.

They both fell into the back seat of their car and Georgie lay back and closed her eyes.

'Tired?' Abe queried and she looked across at him. He still had Tilly in his arms and she had settled against him, her small body floppy in sleep.

'Exhausted.'

'You did very well tonight. I was proud of you.'

'Good.' She turned to stare out of the window even though there was nothing to see because it was pitch black outside now that the bright lights of Basha's palace had been left behind.

She didn't want to talk even though she didn't want the space to be able to think either. She didn't want to give house room to the hurt bubbling inside that she had been practically ignored by Abe for the whole of the evening.

Fatima had long since retired to bed so they both took Tilly up to her bedroom and Georgie began busying herself changing Tilly into pyjamas, aware of Abe hovering in the background and then, eventually, turning on his heel and heading out of the room.

She was yawning as she finally entered the bedroom where Abe, having had a shower, was brushing his teeth, completely naked but for a white towel slung low on his hips and loosely knotted.

He disappeared into the bathroom and emerged a couple of minutes later and strolled towards her.

'You looked lovely in that dress, Georgie, in case I failed to mention it.'

He ran his fingers along the neckline and she drew in a sharp breath, her body responding on cue, nipples tightening, straining against her lacy bra.

He cupped the nape of her neck and pulled her towards him so that his naked chest lightly brushed the silky fall of her evening dress. Of its own wilful accord, Georgie's hand rested against his chest, so hard, so broad and so intensely masculine with its dark hair and flat brown nipples she adored running her tongue over.

She skimmed her fingers along his waist and resisted the temptation to tug the damn towel off him.

She didn't want to do that. She didn't want her thoughts to be obliterated by the feverish, frantic pleasure of sex.

He did that, she realised. His language was the language of sex and he knew how to use it to his greatest advantage, but the unease that had sprung up during the course of the evening wasn't going away and for the first time she wasn't in the mood.

'I'm tired,' she said flatly, spinning around and making straight for the chest of drawers to pull out a nightie.

'Yes, it was a long night,' he acknowledged slowly, suddenly sounding wary.

She didn't answer. She locked the bathroom door behind her, changed into her maiden-aunt nightie and emerged to find him lying in bed with the bedside light on. One arm was folded behind his head and his eyes followed her thoughtfully as she busied herself getting her book and checking her phone before slipping into bed next to him and securing the duvet very firmly around her.

'Are you going to tell me what's wrong or will you stew in silence until the lights get switched off?'

'Nothing's wrong,' she denied curtly.

Abe rolled onto his side to stare at her with a frown. She had seemed at ease this evening, even enjoying herself, he would go so far as to say. Had someone said something to upset her?

'How do you think the evening went?' he asked, trying to draw her out.

'I'm too tired for a conversation, Abe.'

'But not too tired to read?'

'I'm too tired to have sex,' Georgie said bluntly. She shuffled to switch off the light on her side.

He stared at her as she swivelled away and he couldn't help reaching out to manoeuvre her so that she was reluctantly facing him, bodies so close that he could feel the heat emanating from her.

'Is that what I asked?'

'No, but it's what you meant.'

'I thought you seemed to be having a passable time this evening, after the nerves.' He heard the warning bells behind her incendiary statement and chose to ignore them.

'I'm surprised you even noticed, Abe, considering you didn't spend more than five minutes in my company.'

Abe stilled. 'Is that what this is about? The fact that you had to circulate on your own without me holding your hand every step of the way?'

Georgie recoiled, stung. 'I don't expect you to do that, Abe.'

'I realise,' he said, bypassing his discomfort at knowing that he had spoken more harshly than he'd intended, 'that this is all new to you and, believe me, I want to make sure you settle here and find a way of calling it your home, however long that may take.'

'To which end, you're prepared to give me my very own villa, which I can turn into the sort of house I am accustomed to?'

'You think I am being selfish in that?'

'I think you're being considerate, Abe. Considerate and thoughtful, because what other choice do you have?'

'Perhaps we should have this conversation in the

light of day,' he suggested, reaching to turn off his side light, plunging the bedroom into flickering shadows and dark pools.

'You wanted to talk,' Georgie said, more calmly, 'so let's talk. This evening… I finally realised where I am in the pecking order of your life.'

'Extremely high, if you want the truth.'

'No, I'm nowhere near the top. I'm only in it in the first place because of Tilly. You're prepared to do everything within your power to make me feel comfortable here because I'm the mother of your child. But tonight… I realised that, underneath it all, this is a purely business arrangement to you. Yes, I don't doubt that you like me well enough to "rub along nicely", and I don't doubt that you enjoy making love with me, but it's still a business arrangement.'

'Where are you going with this, Georgie? Have I ever misled you on that front? I thought I'd been open and honest about our reasons for marrying from the start. Would you rather I'd lied to you?'

'No. And, no, you haven't misled me. The sad truth is that I ended up misleading myself.' She felt too close to him, his bare chest within touching distance. She sat up abruptly, drew her knees up and folded her arms around them and for a few seconds she buried her head against her knees, just trying to marshal her thoughts.

She wasn't surprised when she felt him getting off the bed and she raised her eyes to follow his progress in the dark. He pulled a chair across so that he was sitting by her side of the bed.

For Abe, she thought, bed equalled sex and this was definitely not the sort of conversation he felt comfortable having between the sheets.

He could compartmentalise brilliantly. His love for his daughter—immediate, instinctual and without compromise—was wonderful but it didn't spill over into his feelings for *her*, for Georgie. Georgie was finally waking up to the reality that she would always and only ever be the duty he had had to take on board as part of the package deal to have his daughter.

The sex was a great bonus but, without it, he would still have offered her exactly the same deal because he would have wanted the same net result.

Georgie knew that they could carry on making love and she could continue to fool herself that what they had might actually end up going somewhere, but tonight had finally opened her eyes to a future that was much more likely. In fact, a future that was downright inevitable.

The problem was that, the more she slept with him, the more blurred the lines between fiction and reality would become.

He saw things through a filter that was purely black and white and that was why their arrangement would work so brilliantly for him.

For her, however…?

'Don't go there, Georgie.' Abe broke the silence, a roughened undertone in his voice.

'I did enjoy tonight,' she said in a low voice. She

couldn't read the expression in his eyes because the room was dark, but she could sense his alertness in his body language. 'Everyone was very nice, and I met people there I hope to get to know better over time. It was nerve-racking to start with, but I settled into it quicker than I thought I would.'

'But…? Because there is a *but* this time, isn't there?'

'I looked for you now and again. I thought you might have shown a bit more interest in my presence. Abe, you were away for two nights…' she dragged in a juddering breath and her eyes locked to his and her heart skipped a beat '…and yet, when you saw me, you didn't even seem that pleased. We were there to do a job and you left me to get on with it because that's the role I've been taken on to fill.'

He sat back, shook his head and raked his fingers through his hair, his movements for once less graceful than usual.

'My apologies,' he said heavily.

'Why would you apologise? Like you said, you never misled me. The fact is that I fell in love with you four years ago in Ibiza and I never stopped. I just never stopped.'

'Don't!'

'You have no idea how devastated I was when I found out that you'd left without telling me…'

'Yes, I do. You have told me countless times but there is only so often I can apologise for the past. It cannot be changed.'

'I realise that! What I'm saying, Abe, is that I

thought all that hurt and bitterness would have protected me against you when you came back into my life. I told you about Tilly and I thought that everything would be reasonably straightforward, that, whatever happened, there was no way you could get to me again, but I was wrong. You did get to me again and tonight it's struck me that everything I feel for you is misplaced because I will never be anything to you but an obligation to bear.'

'That is categorically not true.'

'Then tell me what I mean to you.'

'From what I'm hearing, it would appear not what you're hoping you do.'

'Don't worry; I'm going to go ahead with our arrangement because you're right. Life sometimes entails sacrifices and when it comes to kids, they shouldn't have to pay the price for their parents' mistakes. I can also see with my own two eyes how much you love Tilly, how hard you've tried to gain her trust and, more than that, I can see that Tilly absolutely adores you. But...' she broke out in a film of fine perspiration, knowing that what she next said would determine the course of her life for ever '...no more sex, Abe.' She breathed in deeply. 'From now on, things will have to change between us. You're right, we get along just fine, but we're no longer going to muddy the waters by seeing sex as a bonus.'

Her voice was calm and even. She was proud of herself. How much longer she could maintain the façade was anybody's guess but she knew that she had to get through this next bit, had to dictate her terms and not just go along with the flow because she was in love with him. It had been easy to justify letting her emotions take control of the steering wheel and it was frightening when she thought how long that might have continued if she hadn't had a wake-up call.

He leant towards her with urgency, his dark eyes doing all sorts of unwelcome things to her body, but she held up one hand to stop him in his tracks.

'From now on, we don't share a bed and we lead separate lives until the time comes when Tilly is old enough to understand that not all marriages are made in heaven, and then we can divorce. I know you. You're a man with…desires…but you would have to promise me that you will be discreet.'

'What the hell are you saying, Georgie?'

'I have to protect myself and that starts right now. I don't expect you to remain celibate for me. You can do what you like, and you have my word I will not object.' She looked away. Every word was a shard of glass to her heart but it was for the best. 'I need more emotionally than you have to give and, one day, I know I'll find it. I'm still really young. You do your thing, Abe, and what we have will be what it should have been from the start—a business arrangement with a timeline and a deadline. Now, if you don't mind, I don't want to discuss this any longer. I won't be changing my mind and I don't want you to try to persuade me to. I'm going to go to sleep now and tomorrow…well, tomorrow will be another day…'

CHAPTER TEN

PROMISE NOTHING THAT you can't deliver...spare her the pain of wanting more than you can give...show her how the land lies without varnishing the truth and you'll both be in a better place, where nothing is expected except what's been put on the table...

It had all seemed very straightforward. Abe was well aware that his childhood had set the boundary of his emotional limitations years ago. The prospect of an arranged married had suited him just fine. There would be no risk to his heart, no loss to destroy his soul, and so he had engineered Georgie into the position of accepting the only thing he was making available to her: a marriage based on compatibility and great sex but without love and all its unwelcome complications. He had been upfront with her from the start and then, when he had uneasily suspected that she might have been straying from the straight and narrow, veering into the dangerous, turbulent territory of wanting more than he could ever give, he had tried to pull back, for both their sakes.

Hadn't that been what he had done the night before? Shown her, in not so many words, what their relationship was all about?

Now, glowering at three in the morning in the darkness of his office, brooding over the fact that she had effectively kicked him out of the bedroom, he tried to harness his normally very obedient pragmatism.

He had slung on a pair of loose joggers and a tee shirt and, with his feet on the desk and his leather chair pushed back, he continued to glare through the huge windows out to the darkened, limitless landscape outside.

She wanted more. She wanted love. She wanted the whole fairy-tale story with the happy-ever-after ending and there was no way that he could give her that. He'd already warned her it didn't exist.

He didn't do love! Except for his daughter, his heart was sealed behind a locked door and there was no key to open it up.

Perhaps it was best that all of this had come to a head when it had. She had offered a practical solution to the situation. They would still get married as planned. Tilly's security remained the most important thing and she recognised that as much as he did. Yes, sex would come to an end but perhaps that was a wise decision?

This could be a clean start for them. They would still communicate over what was important and doubtless would remain as compatible in that area as they always had been and if their marriage ended up feeling like a business deal, then wasn't that what it was all about anyway?

She had talked about timelines and deadlines and wasn't that exactly what was needed? A projected way forward with a definite end point? He might be deeply traditional in many ways, and certainly when it came to giving his own flesh and blood the life he knew she deserved, but he was realistic enough to know that relationships didn't necessarily last for ever and if, in the end, Georgie wanted to find love with someone capable of giving it to her, then why shouldn't she once Tilly was old enough for them to work out a suitable arrangement between them?

She had told him that, in essence, he was now a free man. They would marry but he would be able to find physical satisfaction outside wedlock.

He gritted his teeth.

It made all kinds of sense, yes, so why did everything inside him rebel at the prospect?

He pushed himself away from the desk, leapt to his feet and hit the ground running, right back to the bedroom because there was no way this conversation was finished yet.

Georgie was determined to get to sleep. She'd said what she'd wanted to say and the calm of knowing that she had done the right thing had not translated into a peaceful frame of mind.

She had given him permission to stray!

How was that going to play out? How was she going to deal with that? But what other option had she had when she had withdrawn the possibility of them ever sharing a bed together again?

Rather than think about it, she'd dived into her book, but the print had been blurry and her thoughts had been way too busy playing ping-pong for her to do anything other than *think, think, think…*

Eventually, Georgie fell into fitful sleep, so when she heard the bedroom door opening, it took her a few seconds to realise that Abe was back in the room.

She saw the outline of his muscular body framed momentarily in the doorway, backlit by the subdued lighting in the wide corridor outside. He'd changed into clothes but he was barefoot and she was still as he padded across to the bed.

'I know you're awake, Georgie.'

Georgie didn't bother pretending, especially when he followed up that opening remark by perching on the side of the bed.

She flipped over onto her back and shot up so that she was sitting.

'I don't want to talk about this any more, Abe,' she said quietly. 'I've said everything I want to say and now I just want to turn over a new page in this relationship.'

His response was to snap on the bedside light next to her, which made it impossible for her to conceal her expression or fake drowsiness.

'Tell me how you can say that I am not here for you,' he demanded.

'You're not here for me in the way I want you to be. You know exactly what I'm talking about because I told you and I didn't try to hide behind lots of empty words. I want love, Abe, and I deserve it.'

In that instant, Abe realised that sitting on the fence was no longer acceptable. He hadn't even known that that was what he had been doing. He had been protecting himself by suppressing his emotions and he had thought to be protecting *her* as well.

'You tell me that I can have my freedom,' he said gruffly, badly wanting to reach out and touch her, hurting in places he hadn't realised it was possible to hurt, 'and I can't think of anything worse.'

'Well, I'm very sorry to hear that, Abe, but we're finished when it comes to sleeping together. It should never have happened in the first place. I was weak.'

'There's nothing weak about two consenting adults enjoying one another in bed.'

'There is when one of them wants more.'

'Maybe both of them want more,' Abe muttered, suddenly restless and fidgety and stumbling in untried territory.

'What are you trying to say?' Georgie asked bluntly. 'If you think that you can somehow talk me back between the sheets, then it's not going to work. I need to protect myself, Abe, and this is the only way I can do it.'

'That was only ever my wish,' he ventured. 'To protect you.'

He shook his head and looked at her with such blazing sincerity that Georgie briefly averted her eyes, but the pull of his piercing gaze was too compelling. 'I wanted to protect you from…from *me*,' he told her. 'I thought I could never love you the way you needed me to. It wasn't in my make-up, Georgie. Love comes with pain and that was something I learnt from an early age when my mother died.'

'For goodness' sake, Abe,' Georgie cried helplessly, 'that shouldn't be the way it works.' She took a deep breath. 'Nothing is going to convince you otherwise,' she said, 'but my mother also died when I was young, remember? But I didn't let that dictate how I lived the rest of my life.'

'I know.' He half smiled. 'I suppose there was also the onus on me of knowing that one day I would be responsible for running Qaram and, when that time came, there would be no room in my life for the vagaries of love to distract me from doing my duty like it did my father.'

'Which brings us right back to what I told you earlier, Abe. It's over between us. We will provide a united front for Tilly's sake but, beyond that, we will lead our separate lives.'

'I can't do that.'

'Too bad.'

Why not? Georgie was never again going to allow *hope* to determine her behaviour and she firmly squashed all rising tendrils now.

Why was he here? Yes, of course, it was *his* bedroom. It was *his* palace and he could come and go wherever he pleased, but she had asked him to go away and she had meant it and so why was he back?

It wasn't as though he were the sort of heartless creep to override what she wanted. He might not love her, but he was anything *but* a heartless creep.

'You tell me that you want more than…a business arrangement for Tilly's sake. More than just sex. I find that you are not alone in this.'

'What are you trying to say? You're talking in riddles, Abe, and I don't understand.'

'I never stopped to do the maths.' He lowered his head before looking at her once again. 'When I first met you, I never thought it would ever be anything more than a fling. It was how I was programmed to think. I had duties over here and that was all there was to it. We were ships passing in the night. Not telling you who I was seemed like a good idea at the time. Why would I? We've been here before, I know, and we have talked about this, but I met you, Georgie, and I'd never felt more liberated. I outstayed my welcome in Ibiza.' He smiled wistfully. 'Got back here to face the nightmare of my father in hospital and dire warnings to brace myself for the worst. I left thinking I had done the right thing in not saying goodbye, in sparing the inevitable conversation in which I would let you down. Perhaps I even thought that if you were incredibly angry with me and hated me for it, you would recover more quickly.'

'You're right,' she said shortly. 'We've talked about this and I don't want to go over old ground again.'

'Nor do I but I find I must. After you, Georgie, there was precious little on the relationship front…' He sighed and looked at her with such uncharacteristic hesitancy that she had to fight against some treacherous softening.

'Do you honestly think that I'm interested in hearing about what you got up to after we broke up?' she demanded jerkily. 'I'm not!'

'Hear me out, my darling. Please. I'm trying to find words I've never had to find in my life before. I should have been gearing up to marry. My father's early retirement, my taking over the duties of running the country…both those things should have propelled me into the next phase of my life, which was to marry and have children, but I couldn't seem to find the impetus. I know it was a constant source of worry to my father. The necessity of finding a suitable wife was an imperative and, in his depressed frame of mind, he had visions of dying without seeing me wed.' Abe paused. 'No one appealed to me and yet I never joined the dots, never saw the shadow you had cast. Georgie, what I didn't see was that you had managed to set a benchmark that no one else could ever come close to meeting.'

Georgie flushed. Was he lying? Was this some ploy to get her back onside? Surely he couldn't be so cruel?

'Then why didn't you get in touch?' she asked. 'If I set such a high benchmark? Why, Abe?'

'Looking back,' Abe said roughly, 'don't you think I don't realise that that was one of the biggest mistakes of my life? And not because of Tilly, not because I inadvertently missed out on so much, but because of you. Because I fell in love with you over the course of those three weeks and I never recovered. Maybe if I had had some calm in the beginning, I might have sat down and drawn all those conclusions I should have drawn from the start, but I got back to Qaram and then life became turbocharged. I barely had time to sleep, far less think. Or maybe I didn't want to think, didn't want to question everything I had made sure to build into my psyche from a young age.'

Georgie found that she was holding her breath. Her brain was also foggy and the tendrils of hope she had been forcefully shoving down now proliferated at speed.

Had he just said that he had fallen in love with her? Or was her fevered imagination playing tricks?

'It terrifies me, Georgie, to think that I might have continued to sleepwalk into believing that I could be happy without you by my side. I never saw love as part of the business of being married, I never wanted the chaos of being at the mercy of my emotions, but here I am, in love with you and happy to let my emotions chart the direction of my life. I don't want us to be married for convenience. I want us to be married for all those reasons I know you've always believed in. I can only hope that you still believe in them.'

'Oh, Abe.' She smiled and half laughed and pulled him towards her and didn't try to stop her tears. 'With every bit of me, I love you, and I will love you for ever.'

Ibiza. The sun. The azure sea. The turquoise skies above but, this time, no cheap hotel on a packed beach, even though she and Abe had gone right back to the place where they had first met, that buzzing little hotel with its crowded restaurant, the very hotel that had changed her life for ever. After all, this honeymoon was all about paying their nostalgic respects to the place where they had fallen in love, even though it had taken them four years of love lost and then found once again.

Now, she looked out to the infinity pool, where Abe was having fun with Tilly. The orange ball of the setting sun bathed them in a dusky glow. In a minute, they would head inside. The villa behind her was the very height of luxury, befitting royalty. Fatima, here with them, would take over settling Tilly and she and Abe...

She smiled to herself and gazed at the ring on her finger and thought that life could not get any more perfect.

Well...maybe it just about *could*...

On cue, Abe emerged from the pool, Tilly in his arms, sexier and more sinfully striking than any male had a right to be.

'What are you thinking?' he murmured, dipping to briefly kiss her on the mouth.

'I'm thinking we should open some champagne tonight,' Georgie returned as he swapped Tilly over to her before draping her in one of the fluffy white towels.

'I agree.' He slung his arm around her as they made their way inside. 'We need to celebrate the fact that we are here, together and married, because frankly life could not get any better.'

Georgie smiled. She thought back to their wedding a mere six weeks ago. It had been a huge affair, with journalists relishing the exquisite opulence, from the renowned orchestra that provided background music to the sit-down meal, to the ten-metre-long flower tunnel, the blush-pink and ivory flowers imported from Holland. She would remember every second of it and was especially pleased that all her friends from the hotel where she had worked in London had been flown out for the event.

It had been spectacular, as was this honeymoon, which had been delayed to accommodate Tilly's schooling.

Staff were on hand to make sure every need was met but Georgie had earlier given them the evening off. They had their own extensive residence in the grounds at the back but tonight was going to be a night without the lavishly prepared meal.

An hour later, having quickly showered and read a story to Tilly before Fatima took over, Georgie was in the kitchen.

'You're cooking.' Abe smiled, moved towards her and enfolded her in his arms, hands reaching down to cup her buttocks. 'I like that. I like it when you cook. Have I told you that?'

'You have. Many times, my darling.'

They had moved into the villa by the sea, a stone's throw from the palace but light years away in atmosphere. There was none of the formality of an army of staff tending to their every need. It was normality insofar as 'normality' could be categorised as having a top chef cook as and when requested and all cleaning and daily duties done by two girls who came early and left before dusk.

It was also where Georgie had resumed her painting, when she could find time amongst the many duties she had taken on ever since they had married.

'What are we having?' He moved to lift lids off pans and this time she was the one to put her arms around his waist, to rest her head against his back, breathing in his unique smell that could still send her into wonderful meltdown.

'Paella,' she murmured, turning him to face her and looking up into his eyes. 'As befitting where we are. And, of course, champagne, although I may not partake…'

'Tell me more…' He smiled and couldn't stop smiling.

'I don't think I need to, do I?' She tiptoed and kissed him, feeling him still grinning as she drew back, his grin matching hers. 'In approximately eight months' time…you'll be a dad again…'

Abe couldn't think that it was possible to be as happy as he was this very moment. He was with the woman he adored and now they were going to add to their family. He couldn't stop smiling.

'And this time I get to enjoy the experience from the very start. My darling love, I can't wait…'

* * * * *

If you were enchanted by
Desert King's Surprise Love-Child
*how about a dive into these other
Cathy Williams stories?*

Expecting His Billion-Dollar Scandal
The Forbidden Cabrera Brother
Forbidden Hawaiian Nights
Promoted to the Italian's Fiancée
Claiming His Cinderella Secretary

Available now!

#3969 CINDERELLA'S BABY CONFESSION
by Julia James

Alys's unexpected letter confessing to the consequences of their one unforgettable night has ironhearted Nikos reconsidering his priorities. He'll bring Alys to his Greek villa, where he *will* claim his heir. By first unraveling the truth...and then her!

#3970 PREGNANT BY THE WRONG PRINCE
Pregnant Princesses
by Jackie Ashenden

Molded to be the perfect queen, Lia's sole rebellion was her night in Prince Rafael's powerful arms. She never dared dream of more. But now Rafael's stopping her arranged wedding—to claim her and the secret she carries!

#3971 STRANDED WITH HER GREEK HUSBAND
by Michelle Smart

Marooned on a Greek island with her estranged but gloriously attractive husband, Keren has nowhere to run. Not just from the tragedy that broke her and Yannis apart, but from the joy and passion she's tried—and failed—to forget...

#3972 RETURNING FOR HIS UNKNOWN SON
by Tara Pammi

Eight years after a plane crash left Christian with no memory of his convenient vows to Priya, he returns—and learns of his heir! To claim his family, he makes Priya an electrifying proposal: three months of living together...as man and wife.

HPCNMRA1221

#3973 ONE SNOWBOUND NEW YEAR'S NIGHT
by Dani Collins

Rebecca has one New Year's resolution: divorce Donovan Scott. Being snowbound at his mountain mansion isn't part of the plan. And what happens when it becomes clear the chemistry that led to their elopement is still very much alive?

#3974 VOWS ON THE VIRGIN'S TERMS
The Cinderella Sisters
by Clare Connelly

A four-week paper marriage to Luca to save her family from destitution seems like an impossible ask for innocent Olivia... Until he says yes! And then, on their honeymoon, the most challenging thing becomes resisting her irresistible new husband...

#3975 THE ITALIAN'S BARGAIN FOR HIS BRIDE
by Chantelle Shaw

By marrying heiress Paloma, self-made tycoon Daniele will help her protect her inheritance. In return, he'll gain the social standing he needs. Their vows are for show. The heat between them is definitely, maddeningly, *not*!

#3976 THE RULES OF THEIR RED-HOT REUNION
by Joss Wood

When Aisha married Pasco, she naively followed her heart. Not anymore! Back in the South African billionaire's world—as his business partner—she'll rewrite the terms of their relationship. Only, their reunion takes a dangerously scorching turn...

HPCNMRB1221

SPECIAL EXCERPT FROM

ⒽHARLEQUIN
PRESENTS

*Rebecca has one New Year's resolution: divorce
Donovan Scott. Being snowbound at his mountain
mansion isn't part of the plan. And what happens
when it becomes clear the chemistry that led to their
elopement is still very much alive?*

*Read on for a sneak preview of Dani Collins's
next story for Harlequin Presents,*
One Snowbound New Year's Night.

Van slid the door open and stepped inside only to have Becca
squeak and dance her feet, nearly dropping the groceries she'd
picked up.

"You knew I was here," he insisted. "That's why I woke you, so
you would know I was here and you wouldn't do that. I *live* here,"
he said for the millionth time, because she'd always been leaping
and screaming when he came around a corner.

"Did you? I never noticed," she grumbled, setting the bag on the
island and taking out the milk to put it in the fridge. "I was alone
here so often, I forgot I was married."

"*I* noticed that," he shot back with equal sarcasm.

They glared at each other. The civility they'd conjured in
those first minutes upstairs was completely abandoned—probably
because the sexual awareness they'd reawakened was still hissing
and weaving like a basket of cobras between them, threatening to
strike again.

Becca looked away first, thrusting the eggs into the fridge along
with the pair of rib eye steaks and the package of bacon.

She hated to be called cute and hated to be ogled, so Van tried
not to do either, but *come on*. She was curvy and sleepy and wearing
that cashmere like a second skin. She was shorter than average and
had always exercised in a very haphazard fashion, but nature had
gifted her with a delightfully feminine figure-eight symmetry. Her

ample breasts were high and firm over a narrow waist, then her hips flared into a gorgeous, equally firm and round ass. Her fine hair was a warm brown with sun-kissed tints, her mouth wide, and her dark brown eyes positively soulful.

When she smiled, she had a pair of dimples that he suddenly realized he hadn't seen in far too long.

"I don't have to be here right now," she said, slipping the coffee into the cupboard. "If you're going skiing tomorrow, I can come back while you're out."

"We're ringing in the New Year right here." He chucked his chin at the windows that climbed all the way to the peak of the vaulted ceiling. Beyond the glass, the frozen lake was impossible to see through the thick and steady flakes. A gray-blue dusk was closing in.

"You have four-wheel drive, don't you?" Her hair bobbled in its knot, starting to fall as she snapped her head around. She fixed her hair as she looked back at him, arms moving with the mysterious grace of a spider spinning her web. "How did you get here?"

"Weather reports don't apply to me," he replied with self-deprecation. "Gravity got me down the driveway and I won't get back up until I can start the quad and attach the plow blade." He scratched beneath his chin, noted her betrayed glare at the windows.

Believe me, sweetheart. I'm not any happier than you are.

He thought it, but immediately wondered if he was being completely honest with himself.

"How was the road?" She fetched her phone from her purse, distracting him as she sashayed back from where it hung under her coat. "I caught a rideshare to the top of the driveway and walked down. I can meet one at the top to get back to my hotel."

"Plows will be busy doing the main roads. And it's New Year's Eve," he reminded her.

"So what am I supposed to do? Stay here? All night? With *you*?"

"Happy New Year," he said with a mocking smile.

Don't miss
One Snowbound New Year's Night.
*Available January 2022 wherever
Harlequin Presents books and ebooks are sold.*

Harlequin.com

HE WHO HESITATES . . . DIES!

Simultaneously, with his left hand reaching around to insert the key into the lock, Dusty's right crossed to slip the Colt from his near-side holster. Then he timed the cocking of the hammer with the turning of the key so that the two sets of clicking sounded together.

Dusty twisted the doorknob and shoved hard. He went across the threshold in a fast dive.

The room was occupied.

But there were two intruders, not one.

Opposite the door, a man was sitting on the sill of the open window, holding a sawed-off shotgun with its twin barrels aligned at what would have been chest height on a person of average size entering the room. The second intruder was to the right. Apparently he had been examining the contents of the wardrobe.

For all his readiness, the man at the window appeared to be surprised to see who was coming in. Instead of trying to correct his point of aim immediately, he stared at the small Texan in amazement. His companion duplicated his reaction, his right hand dipping toward the butt of a holstered Army Colt.

Such hesitation was fatal when dealing with a gunfighter of Dusty Fog's caliber . . .

Also by J.T. Edson

COLD DECK, HOT LEAD